# Seasons of the Heart

## Kay D. Rizzo

**Pacific Press Publishing Association**
Boise, Idaho
Oshawa, Ontario, Canada

Edited by Marvin Moore
Designed by Tim Larson
Cover by Eric Joyner
Type set in 10/10 Korinna

**Library of Congress Catalog Card Number: 87-42567**

ISBN 0-8163-0703-2

87 88 89 90 91 ● 5 4 3 2 1

# Contents

# Chapter 1
# Wisconsin Interlude

Kari threw the tattered canvas-sided suitcase onto the bed and yanked at the closure. "This impossible buckle! I can't get it undone," she sobbed. Tears blurred her vision. Blindly, she pawed around the rim of the bag, trying to locate the zipper pull. "I've got to get out of here. Oh please, Lord, help me to open this stupid case!"

As her left hand settled over the zipper pull, Kari sensed the presence of an intruder. She whirled about to face him. "What are you doing in here? Haven't you done enough damage for one lifetime?"

Keith, her third stepfather, snickered and leaned against the doorjamb. "She won't believe you, you know. Her pride won't let her. Sheena needs me far more than she ever needed a daughter." An unlit cigarette hung limp and insolent from his mouth. "Too bad she had to show up when she did. You and me could have had some fun. Of course your religion wouldn't have allowed that, would it?"

Kari backed away from him, her eyes spitting anger. "You stay away from me, do you hear? I'm not some simpering child you can molest at will."

"Ooh," Keith sneered, "the pretty kitten's showing her claws!"

Kari clamped her jaw shut, hurried to her dresser, grabbed a handful of clothing, and tossed it into the open case.

Again Keith sneered. "You gonna run to your do-gooder buddy?"

Kari stuffed another armload of clothing into the case. "You leave Amanda Fisher and her family out of this."

"Hmmph!" Keith snorted, stretching out his arms to effectively bar the doorway. "You'll be back, you know. You can't resist. And I'll be waiting."

Kari continued packing her belongings until she'd stuffed the last handful of clothing into the case. Then she zipped it closed, grabbed the case by the handle, threw her coat over one arm, and started for the door. "Let me by!" she ordered.

"And what if I don't?" Keith tipped his head to one side and grinned.

Kari shuddered. Keith's uneven, stained, fanglike teeth had always reminded her of a reptile. "Do you really want to find out?" Kari eyed him malevolently.

A voice from the dining room broke the moment of challenge. "Keithy baby, is my good-for-nothing daughter trying to lure you into her bedroom again?" Sheena, her streaked blond hair straggling across her flushed cheek, her eyes watering and bloodshot, staggered to one side, beer can in hand. Sheena flew into a tirade when she spotted Kari in the doorway. "You cheap little tramp, didn't I tell you to get out of my house? Trying to take my man from me! That's what you were doing." Sheena aimed her body in the general direction of the parlor and stumbled forward, arms outstretched to steady herself.

"Is that what that no-account church is teaching you? Them and their so called principles! Teaching a girl to turn against her loving mother? I should report 'em to the police." Pointing weakly toward Kari, she continued. "And—and the Amanda whats-her-name too."

"Mother," Kari began, watching Sheena cringe at the title of mother, "I am certain that somewhere in the alcohol-deadened recesses of your mind you know what really happened here today."

Keith jumped to attention. "Nothin' happened, Sheena baby. Don't let her kid ya'. You know that you're my one and only."

Kari continued, ignoring his protestations. "In times past, when you've thrown me out, I've come crawling back. But now, thanks to Amanda Fisher and to my faith in God, I can stand on my own two feet, which is more than you can say. If you ever decide to rid yourself of this—this parasite you call a husband, let me know."

For a moment, Sheena swayed, her eyes clouding over as if she would fall into a drunken stupor. Keith stepped to Sheena's side, draped an arm across her shoulders, and sneered. "Well, if you're going . . . "

"Yeah, get out! Get out of my house! And never come back," Sheena screeched. Furrows of pain filled Kari's brow for an instant. Then she closed her eyes, took a deep breath, and left the apartment.

Mrs. Dumont, the building superintendent's wife, stood at the base of the stairs, broom in hand, shaking her head sadly. "Goodbye Kari. My Joey and Jeremy will miss you."

Kari flushed, knowing that the cheerful little round-faced woman had heard every word. "Thanks, Mrs. Dumont. Tell the twins goodbye for me, won't you?" The woman nodded and attacked a corner of dust under the stairwell with her broom.

Weighted down with emotions too heavy to handle, Kari barely noticed the shabby little shops, the boarded-up store windows, and the graffiti-covered brick walls on her way to Amanda's apartment. Even knowing that Amanda would happily open her hide-a-bed and her home to Kari, she hated to inconvenience the young widow again. "Maybe it's time," Kari thought, "to take Amanda up on that offer to spend the summer in Wisconsin helping her older sister. With the nurses all out on strike, I don't stand a chance of landing a job right away. Yeah, maybe Wisconsin's the best bet for me right now. What do you think, Lord?"

Just as Kari had predicted, Amanda swept the young woman into her home, brushing aside all of Kari's apologies. "I won't hear any more about it, Kari. You and I are past that stage in our friendship, right? A sister in Christ can do no less."

Kari's eyes misted over. "You're too good to me."

Amanda laughed and handed Kari a set of sheets and pillowcases. "Ho! I plan to put you to work tonight babysitting the kids. I was wondering what I would do. The agency called me this morning. They want me to work the graveyard shift again."

Amanda bustled into the parlor, opening the hide-a-bed and chatting along the way. Kari followed with the bedding. "Is your sister's offer still open? You know, for someone to help her this summer?"

Amanda's eyebrows lifted quizzically. "I thought you didn't want to give farm life a try."

Kari grinned, shrugging her shoulders. "Maybe I was too hasty."

Amanda nodded and frowned, hesitating before she spoke. "You've been through a lot today. Don't make a decision until you've had enough time to pray about it and be certain God is leading you that way. We could start by praying right now," Amanda suggested.

Kari agreed, immediately kneeling down beside the extended hide-a-bed. Amanda joined her, and in turn they prayed that Kari would have faith that God would take care of her and that she would learn to forgive her mother and Keith. When they rose from their knees, Kari threw her arms around Amanda's neck. "Thanks. Thanks for just being here."

Kari picked up a large pillow and threw it onto the sofa, then stared at the abstract design in the carpet. She knew Amanda was right, but with very little cash and no immediate prospects of employment, and with the ink on her practical nursing license barely dry, Kari also knew that time was not on her side. She eyed her friend. "If the Lord has an alternate plan, I'll need to know it soon."

Amanda bent over to tuck in the last corner of the light-weight blanket. "In His good time, Honey, in His good time."

Three days later Kari's eyes sparkled with anticipation as she stared out the train window at the scattered lights from farms and villages racing by in the night. She ran her fingers over the broad, green upholstered seats that had seemed so cushiony when she boarded the passenger car earlier in Chicago. Now they felt scratchy and confining.

For the first time since it happened, the memories of her last few days in Chicago seemed mercifully blurred in her mind. She glanced about the passenger car, empty except for an elderly woman seated to her right and a middle-aged man, disheveled from travel, sitting two rows ahead of her. Kari idly wondered where her traveling companions might be going and what adventures they'd face upon arriving at their destination. "Will their lives change as much as mine?"

"I don't understand myself at all, " she mused, her lips talking soundlessly to her reflection in the windowpane. "One minute I'm as anxious as a ten-year-old heading for Lake Michigan on a hot July day; and the next, I feel alone, totally alone, almost like that—that water tower." She stared after the light blinking on the tower silhouetted on the horizon until it disappeared from view, then shook her head and sighed.

An all-too-familiar chill prickled at the nape of Kari's neck. "Can I survive without Amanda's strength, without her unfaltering faith in God, without her wise counsel?" She leaned back against the seat and closed her eyes, finally forcing her mind to transport her south across the rolling farmlands, past the ramshackle, soot-clothed shanties along the tracks, to Chicago's south side and to Amanda Fisher's three room walk-up apartment.

It was there, after receiving months of Amanda's unwarranted compassion, understanding, and love, that Kari caught her first glimpse of Jesus. There, one cold February night in the tiny efficiency kitchen, Kari stood before a sinkful of dirty dishes and came face-to-face with Amanda's Saviour.

Kari's discovery hadn't been due to one encounter, one hymn, or one sermon. It came after months of listening to Amanda share how God had led in her life, even through the death of her minister husband, and observing Amanda's behavior in the very unchristian world of south Chicago. It was Kari's admiration of Amanda's buoyant spirit, as the young woman struggled to maintain a full-time job at the state welfare agency and bring up her two children alone, that finally broke the girl's resistance.

Yet every time Kari attempted to tell Amanda how much she admired her, Amanda recoiled and shook her head vigorously. "Oh no, Kari. Please don't. Without Jesus I am a weakling. Look to Jesus—He's who you want to copy."

The train whistle jarred Kari out of her reverie as they passed through another sleeping Wisconsin town. She slipped her feet from her high-heeled sandals and curled them under her in the double seat. Idly, she massaged her stockinged toes and eased back into her memories.

She'd met Amanda one frigid February night when she wandered into a neighborhood church during a Wednesday night prayer-meeting service. Seventeen years old at the time, Kari had fled from her mother's drunken tirade, trudging aimlessly through the subzero, snow-crusted streets until she stopped in front of the brightly lighted church.

The building looked so warm and inviting. The sound of four-part harmony drifted out to where she shivered beneath the streetlight. With nothing else to do and no place else to go, Kari climbed the steps to the church and stepped inside.

Tears threatened to melt Kari's facade midway through Pastor Mason's sermon on the unfaltering love of God. Dabbing the corners of her eyes with her fingertips, she slipped out of the pew and through the swinging doors to the vestibule, unaware that the gentle-faced woman who earlier had shared a tattered song book with her, followed her.

"Amanda." Kari thought as the train swayed back and forth over the rails. "Leave it to her to immediately sense when someone needed her special brand of love, and then refuse to take No for an answer."

Growing up in one of the roughest neighborhoods of Chicago, Kari had never met anyone like the amazing Amanda Fisher. After a bowl of hot stew and a good night's sleep on Amanda's hide-a-bed, Kari's barriers crumbled. From then on, Amanda became Kari's hero. When Amanda suggested that Kari take the licensed practical nurse course at the local hospital, Kari signed up. So many times during the months that followed, Kari was tempted to quit, but Amanda always managed to talk her into staying with the program for at least one more quarter.

Sheena, her mother, threw Kari out of the apartment on a reccuring basis. Amanda and the children always took Kari in. Then, when Sheena would beg Kari to come back home, she would leave again, only to repeat the pattern a month or two later. It was Keith who finally severed the cord. Kari knew now that she could never go home again.

Somewhere along the way, Kari imagined herself the opposite of the little boy in the Hans Christian Anderson story who stopped the flood waters behind the crumbling dike with his finger. Amanda's touch unleashed a flood of hurts in Kari that allowed her to heal.

An abrupt snort and cough from the sleeping man two rows ahead of her interrupted her woolgathering. Kari yawned and stretched her feet in front of her, then curled up in the seat again to restring her memories. "So much has changed. Who would have thought, because of a chance meeting more than two years ago, that I'd find myself a baptized Christian, a licensed practical nurse, and on a train heading for the farm lands of Wisconsin?"

The coach lights dimmed, then brightened as the monotonous clicketyclack of the wheels changed pace, signaling the train's approach to a station. A rotund, flushed-faced conductor bellowed his way through the coach without missing a beat. "Columbus, Wisconsin. Columbus, Wisconsin. Those deboarding should have their luggage claim checks available for the porter upon reaching the platform."

Kari swallowed the sudden lump in her throat. "No! I won't be scared! I won't feel sorry for myself. I'm not abandoned. I'm not alone. God and I will make it—together. I'm a fighter. I'm a survivor!" She lifted her chin and tightened her lips, determined to defeat her own self-pity. "OK, Lord, I suppose turning me into a country hick should be easy enough after all the other changes You've made in my life."

The brakes squealed, and the train jerked and hissed to a stop. With a stubborn resolve, Kari slipped her raincoat over her arm, stuffed the fashion magazines she'd purchased during the Milwaukee stopover into her red sports bag, and stood up. She turned to grasp both seatbacks firmly and noticed an elderly woman behind her struggling with her packages.

"Excuse me, Ma'am, but do you need any help?"

The woman's faced crinkled into a smile. "Oh, do I!" she replied, heaving a huge sigh of relief. "That would be so nice of you. My niece, Betty, will be here at the station to meet me, if you could just help me onto the platform."

"Glad to." Kari grabbed two of the bulging shopping bags by their handles and slipped one of the white bakery boxes under her arm.

The old lady's eyes danced with delight as she pointed to the box. "That one's for Betty. She used to love Wiedelbaum's fresh-baked bagels. I even brought her some genuine dills from the deli down my block. Nothing's quite as good as pickles from a barrel, don't you agree?"

"Yes, Ma'am." Kari sidled up the aisle toward the exit sign ahead of the woman, the packages catching on each seat she passed.

"Is someone meeting you? A young girl like yourself shouldn't be waiting around a depot at this hour of the night." The woman clucked merrily after Kari as she stepped onto the platform. A porter standing at the base of the steps released Kari's arm to assist the older woman.

"Now, don't you worry. It's not that late, and I'm certain someone will be here momentarily. The train is a trifle early," Kari reminded, her eye singling out a brisk, carefully dressed matron hurrying toward them. "Perhaps this is Mrs. Wynters," Kari thought, then reconsidered. "I hope not, considering the frown she's wearing!"

"There you are, Aunt Mabel. Tsk! I thought I told you not to bring half of Chicago with you. You know that Harold and I don't eat such rich foods anymore." The interloper whisked the bags and packages from the suddenly silent old woman. "Now what will we do with all of this? I really wish you'd listen to me." Kari watched the old woman's eyes flash with embarrassment, then dull with a resolute sadness. Somehow the woman had aged at least ten years before Kari's eyes. Kari smiled sympathetically. "Excuse me, but don't forget these packages also." Kari gently placed them in the older woman's limp arms.

The niece snatched at the bags. "More? You brought more junk? Here, give them to me!" She ordered. "A waste of good money!" The woman glanced past Kari as if she were invisible. Kari watched the older woman struggle to follow her smartly stepping niece into the crowded station.

"Hmm!" She muttered, "What a nasty person!"

"Who's nasty?" An unfamiliar voice interrupted her thoughts.

# Chapter 2
# Marc Wynters

Kari's mouth gaped open and her cheeks reddened. She whirled about to find herself face-to-face with the third button of a well-filled blue denim shirt. Slowly, Kari lifted her startled eyes to face a grinning, dimpled, blond giant of a man.

"Excuse me, but you *are* Kari Gerard, aren't you?" The young man's eyes sparkled, as if only he knew the punch line to some hilarious joke. "You do look like your picture, you know—the one Aunt Amanda sent?"

"Um, oh yes. I'm Kari, but who are you?" Frightened that her preadolescent reaction to the man might be obvious, she fought to regain her composure. For no apparent reason, she could feel herself blushing again. "Be still, my beating heart!" She scolded herself silently. "This guy can't be for real. They only build custom design models like this one in Hollywood!" Her gaze perused the slight cleft in his chin, the strong pulsing throb in his throat, a set of bulging muscles barely concealed by the rolled-up chambray sleeves.

"I'm sorry. I guess I startled you. Of course you wouldn't know me. Let's begin again." He extended a bronzed, weathered hand. "Good evening. My name is Marc Wynters. You must be Kari Gerard."

Kari took a deep breath. "Why yes, I am. It is so nice to meet you, Mr. Wynters, and so kind of you to escort me to your parents' home."

"Not at all," he teased. "I'm the family gofer—go fer this and go fer that. Seriously, Mom and Dad had a board meeting at the church tonight and asked me to do the honors. So here I am, at your service. You have luggage?"

"Oh yes, just a minute." Kari fumbled through her purse for the baggage claim tickets she'd stuffed inside her wallet earlier when she'd offered to help the elderly woman with her packages. "Ah, here they are." She held them up victoriously.

"I'll get the luggage for you." Marc took the tickets from her hands. "Do you drive?"

11

"I'm afraid not. Living in Chicago all of my life I've not had reason or opportunity to learn." Kari hurried to keep up with him, trying to match her high-heeled stride to that of the tall farm boy. "Boy?" she mused. "Hardly!"

"Have you eaten? I'm starved! There's a diner here in town where we can get something." Marc rambled on, oblivious to her silence. "Mom was afraid that I'd miss you, so she hurried me through my dinner. No seconds!" Marc laughed and guided her through the crowd.

"Perhaps a sandwich would be nice," Kari admitted. "Dutch treat, however."

"Nonsense! When I ask a girl out, I expect to cover all expenses." He stopped and pointed at her white patent-leather strapped heels. "Those shoes weren't made for walking. Why don't you wait here while I get the pickup truck? I'm parked quite a ways out."

While waiting for Marc's return, Kari became fascinated with the swirls and curlicues on the baroque ornamentation of the railway station, a relic from an earlier era. When a voice called to her, she glanced over her shoulder.

"Hey, cutie, wanna' party?" A battered green Chevy jerked up to the curb. Its driver leaned across the tattered front seat. "Hop in. I'll show ya' the sights of Columbus. How about it?"

Accustomed to big city mashers, Kari had learned early to ignore the catcalls and lewd invitations one received from cruising drivers. "The weirdos are out in force tonight," she mumbled, her brow knitting into a heavy scowl. She could hear the car roar off to hunt for a more cooperative female. "Nothing changes. Whether it's Chicago or small town U.S.A., the same scum prowl for easy prey."

"Hey, I don't like to be ignored, sweetie." A greasy-looking guy hopped out of a rundown sports car parked alongside the curb and sauntered toward her.

"Beat it. I'm not interested," she warned, her left eyebrow arching in disgust. She returned her attention to the marble carvings over the front entrance of the depot.

"Aw, come on. I can show you a real good time. You're a classy dame. Don't be so uppity."

Though she refused to look toward him, Kari could sense the stranger had moved within arms' reach. She held her breath and hurried toward the depot.

"You heard the lady," a familiar voice drawled. "She said to get lost. And that's just what you want to do, right?"

Relieved beyond belief, Kari choked back a giggle as she whirled to watch her towering rescuer, thumbs firmly thrust into his belt loops, stare down the suddenly cowardly masher.

Marc grasped the smaller man's shoulders and grinned. "Now friend, don't you think it's time you got back into your car and took a nice long drive?"

"Right! Sounds good! Sorry man. No offense. I didn't know she was your chick. Sorry, lady. Hey, stay cool, man. Everything's cool." The stranger edged around his vehicle and into the driver's seat. Gunning all the power at his command, he roared off, disappearing down the street in a cloud of exhaust fumes.

"Don't you know how to handle creeps like that?" Marc growled.

Kari leaped to her own defense. "Of course I do. Chicago's polluted with them. Besides, I didn't encourage him in the slightest. I usually don't make it a habit to be out on the street at this time of night."

"You're right. It was my fault for leaving a pretty girl alone in the first place. I should have known better. I apologize. Here, get in." He opened the passenger door of the pickup.

Marc glanced from Kari's navy blue, straight skirt and high heeled pumps to the knee-high step into the truck. Grasping her about the waist, he lifted her into the cab. Breathless, Kari stammered an awkward Thank you and straightened the skirt about her knees.

Catching a glimpse of herself in the rear-view mirror, she gasped. "I'm a mess." She opened her purse and removed a small silver compact, the compact Amanda and the children had given her the previous Christmas. Though she knew the message engraved on the bottom of the compact by heart, she read it again for strength.

"Favour is deceitful, and beauty is vain: but a woman that feareth the Lord, she shall be praised. Proverbs 31:30. Kari's birthday text— August 30."

Looking in the mirror, she whispered, "Lord, I may never be beautiful, but I will always praise You." She brushed aside a stray black curl from her cheek. "Praising You is all that's worth anything in this world anyway." She frowned, trying to push back painful memories that threatened to surface.

Kari's own insecurities prevented her from seeing what others saw when they looked at her. But these same insecurities did nothing to cloud any man's view, including Marc's. Kari's jade green eyes formed a perfect relief for her flawless, creamy complexion, touched with a natural blush. Her face, more comely than stunning, was dramatically outlined by jet black tresses that swirled casually around her shoulders. Her pert upturned nose added a hint of defiance. However, when Kari viewed herself in the mirror, all she saw were tired eyes, smudged makeup, and hopelessly tangled curls.

Marc hopped into the cab, drove a few blocks, and stopped in front of a small, brightly lighted cafe. "I'm afraid Duke's Diner will have to do. Everything else is closed for the day." Mark stepped into the street, walked around the cab, and opened her door. Again, before she could protest, he grasped her about the waist and lowered her to the sidewalk. With his hands still about her waist, he hesitated. "Did you know that my two hands can completely encircle your waist? Incredible!" He mumbled, shaking his head.

After they had settled into a quiet booth at the back of the diner and the waitress had taken their orders, Kari searched for impersonal topics to discuss: the weather, her trip to Wisconsin, a sixth-grade science field trip she'd once taken to Michigan.

Though the diner lacked in romantic atmosphere, the soft flickering light from the luau candle in the center of the table encouraged Marc to open up more. "I'm in my last year of veterinary medicine at the Michigan State University. I'll be glad when it's over. I love farming, but making a decent living at it these days—well, it's mighty difficult. So I figured I might be able to run a farm if I also doctored animals on the side." He laughed at his obvious joke.

Even Kari knew that no one became a veterinarian as a side profession. The course involved long years of study equal to that of a medical doctor. Marc leaned back against the booth. "And what about you, Kari Gerard? What are your plans for the future?"

"I—I'm not sure right now. I've just completed my LPN course, and I had planned on working at a hospital near my home in Chicago. But plans change, so here I am." She chuckled a bit, then went on. "Once, long ago, before I found Christ, I considered becoming a fashion designer." The waitress momentarily interrupted their conversation by placing their food in front of them. Kari grimaced when the waitress grinned and winked at Marc. "Will that be all?" she asked.

Marc assured her it would be, and politely brushed her obvious advances aside. "Back to where we were. A fashion designer? Hmm. I'm sure that God can use the witness of a fashion designer as well as that of a nurse. Everyone isn't called to become a missionary to Africa, you know. Think of the population explosion the African continent would have if we all went there."

"Oh, I know that, but thanks to your Aunt Amanda, I discovered I enjoy helping people in a more direct manner. I couldn't have finished the training if Amanda hadn't encouraged me so," Kari answered. She looked up from her French fries and flushed with discomfort as her eyes met his.

After all the trouble she'd had with her mother's latest husband, Keith, Kari had vowed never to complicate her life by trusting a man. "And now," she thought, "this guy comes along with the teasingest blue eyes I've ever seen, demanding my attention. Maybe coming to Wisconsin wasn't such a good idea after all, Lord."

Kari followed Marc's lead of bowing his head for a quick blessing. She still found it difficult to pray in a public place. When she raised her head, Marc continued with his questioning. "So why did you come to Wisconsin?"

She thought for a moment, then replied. "I guess I needed space and time. Time to think and get my life together."

He leaned back and laughed. "Space we have—miles of it. But time?" He asked incredulously. "You expect to find time to think on a farm? In the summer? The only time you'll likely have to think will be when you fall into your bed at night. By then, you'll be so tired you'll think sleep instead."

"I'm sure I have lots to learn, Mr. Wynters." She lifted her nose and arched one brow. Her fingers tapped out her impatience on the red Formica table top.

"Hey, don't be offended. I wasn't laughing at you. You're young, inexperienced. I'm sure you'll find lots of time to think." Marc slipped the check into his hand, slid a handful of coins beneath the rim of the saucer, and reached for Kari's hand to help her from the booth.

"Please, I prefer to pay my own way." She deftly removed her hand from his grasp.

"No way!" The warm blue of Marc's eyes turned steely gray. "I told you my policy on that subject. It's not open for discussion at this time. Now, may I assist you?"

Still stinging from his patronizing references to her age and inexperience, Kari bristled. "I certainly would not cause a scene, and I am also certain that I can manage without your help, thank you." She threw him a saccharin sweet smile and strolled out of the restaurant.

She muttered all the way across the parking lot to the truck. "If he thinks I'll be a simpering mouse and ooh and aah over his masculinity, he's quite mistaken! Hmpf, egotistical know-it-all! Just like every other man I've ever met. For a moment I thought he'd be different. Huh! Just goes to show, Kari Gerard, how wrong you can be." She sniffed and folded her arms defiantly. "He'll obviously be no threat to my anti-male vow, no threat at all."

She yanked the cab door open and eyed the step critically. "This is stupid. Any jerk can climb into the cab of a truck, right? Wrong!" Kari admitted, analyzing the problem further. "Well, I'll just kick off my heels and hike my skirt to the knees and—"

Two strong hands again encircled her waist and lifted her onto the seat.

"Hey, what do you think you're doing?" Humiliated, Kari straightened her skirt and her dignity. "I said I could do it myself!" she sputtered.

"Yeah, and give those truckers over there a Parisian revue?" Marc slammed her door, stomped around the truck and climbed in behind the wheel. "Women!" He muttered.

Kari shot him a defiant glance.

# Chapter 3
# A New Family

Marc swung the pickup truck down a narrow dirt road shrouded with trees, stopping before a massive, two-story Victorian farmhouse. Kari could make out the vague shadows of a gingerbread trim along the eaves of the porch.

"Well, here we are. I'll get your luggage." Marc hopped out, rounded the truck, and opened her door. Again, before she could protest, he whisked her from the seat.

"Ready or not, you're about to meet the entire clan. That is, all except Shelly, my big sister. She got married last February." He grinned. "You'll meet her soon enough." A high pitched shriek greeted Kari as ten-year-old Mindy burst through the screen door onto the brightly lighted porch.

"She's here, Mom," Mindy squealed. "She's really here!" Kari could make out the shadow of a teenage boy veiled by the screen door.

"The whole world knows now, Mindy," Marc teased, tugging on his younger sister's platinum ponytail. "I'll bet Grandma Lewis heard your transmission this time, and she lives over a half mile away. Others might use a telephone or a telegraph, but the Wynters have tell-a-Mindy."

Mindy stuck out her tongue defiantly at her older brother.

"Hi, Mindy." Kari stepped nervously on the the porch to greet the young girl.

The screen door squeaked again as Michael joined Kari and Mindy on the porch.

"Kari, this is my dumb brother Michael," Mindy said. "I'm so glad you're here. Now I have a fighting chance against these two bullies."

"Hi, Michael. Does anyone ever call you Mike?" Kari asked, smiling up into the husky fifteen-year-old boy's blushing face.

"Yeah, once in a while, I guess." He turned to his older brother. "Marc, I'll grab the other bag," he mumbled, obviously anxious to escape center stage.

"Here, let me carry your travel case," Mindy said. "We've been waiting all day for you to arrive." She bounced ahead two steps to Kari's one. "I

16

wanted to meet you at the train but Mom insisted I stay here to answer the phone in case anything went wrong with your schedule."

Kari stepped back down the porch steps momentarily and surveyed her new home. "It's perfect. Just like I thought it would look!"

"Huh? What's perfect?" Mindy spun around trying to spot the object of Kari's attention.

"The white house, the porch, the swing. Does the porch go all the way around the house? It's just like something from 'The Waltons' reruns," Kari exclaimed.

Mindy frowned. "The porch stops just beyond the back door, and we're not the Waltons."

"Sure we are," Marc interrupted. "I've always wanted to be the famous John-Boy."

"Yeah, and I'm Jim-Bob. Mindy, you can be Elizabeth," Michael teased.

"No way!" Mindy rose to the bait.

"I'm sorry, Mindy, but I did mean it as a compliment," Kari interjected.

"Don't pay any attention to her," Marc drawled. "Lately, she's too sophisticated for the likes of us country folk." A grin teased the corners of his mouth. "Come on. Let's go inside and meet the rest of the family."

The frightening moment had arrived. Would Mr. and Mrs. Wynters like her? Would they accept her, give her a chance? Suddenly fear overwhelmed Kari. "I will never leave you, nor forsake you," she whispered as she fortified her courage. Setting her jaw firmly, she took a deep breath and crossed the threshold into the front room.

"Welcome, child. Come on in here. Let me get a good look at you." A large, comfortable arm encircled Kari's shoulders and drew her into the soft, incandescent light of the parlor. "We're so glad you got here all right. I didn't like the idea of your traveling alone all the way from Chicago, but my little sister Mandy knows best." Kari looked up into Mrs. Wynters' round face, aglow with friendliness.

"Mandy?" Kari thought. "Who's Mandy?" Then suddenly she understood. "Of course, Mom Amanda is Mrs. Wynters' sister."

Kari started at the sound of a strong bass voice behind her. "She's such a little thing. She looks like she could blow away with the first strong wind. I hope farm life won't be too rough for her." Kari turned to see a giant of a man with blond hair, graying at the temples, and with Marc's wide, friendly smile. Mr. Wynters extended his hand.

The woman patted Kari's arms. "Don't tease now. She'll do just fine." Mrs. Wynters turned toward the boys standing in the doorway with the luggage. "Take Kari's suitcases up to her room, boys. And Kari, sit down beside me and tell me all about your trip."

Mrs. Wynters led the nervous young woman to a brown, worn sofa lined with a wild array of colorful throw pillows. "Dad and I would have come for you ourselves, but we had a church board meeting we couldn't miss."

"That's OK. Marc was good company." Kari cleared her throat uncomfortably.

Mrs. Wynter looked first at Kari, than at Marc. A frown threatened to cross her brow, which she quickly replaced with a congenial smile. "I'm glad all went well," she added. "When I complained to Amanda about how much I miss my oldest daughter's help since her marriage last February, she mentioned that she knew of a young woman who could use a home for the summer. And that's what this is"—Mrs. Wynters gestured about the room—"your home."

Kari's broad smile didn't completely hide the uncertainty she knew was revealed in her eyes. "Thank you, Mrs. Wynters. I really appreciate your invitation. And I'm used to hard work, I promise, in spite of my size. My instructors during nurses' training made sure of that."

Mom Wynters patted Kari's arm again. "Now wait a minute. First, call me Mom, and Marcus here is Dad. We'll feel more comfortable that way, and so will you. Second, while you're with us, you're part of the family. You don't need to work any harder than the rest of us. On a farm, in the summertime, there's enough work for everyone. And let's pray that your nursing skills won't be necessary around here right away."

"Speaking of work," Dad Wynters interrupted, "a new day of chores begins in only a few hours, boys. We'd better have worship and get to bed." He gestured as Marc and Michael returned from taking Kari's luggage to her room.

"Aw, Dad," Michael groaned, glancing toward Kari and blushing again.

"We have all summer to get acquainted," Mom Wynters reminded. "And I'm sure Kari is more than tired after her long trip. Gather round."

Dad Wynters picked up a large brown Bible and settled himself in a recliner. "I'll keep it short tonight. We're all tired."

After Dad Wynters read from Psalm 1, they formed a circle and joined hands while Dad prayed. Kari stood in awe at the flurry of kisses and hugs passed around between the family members after prayer. Mom Wynters noticed the girl's surprise and quickly planted a goodnight kiss on Kari's cheek.

"Let me show you to your room, dear," Mom Wynters said. "I've put you in Shelly's room. If there are any cool breezes on these hot summer nights, you'll feel them in that room." Kari giggled nervously at the sight of the entourage climbing the stairs.

"Boys, off to bed. Mindy, you too," Mom ordered as she opened the door to Kari's new room. She stepped inside. "Well, here we are. Everything's springtime fresh and waiting for you. You can put your clothes in the bureau and in the closet over there. There should be enough hangers. If not, there are plenty more downstairs in the hall closet." Mom Wynters bustled about the room as she talked.

Overwhelmed, Kari stood in the doorway trying to catch all of the woman's instructions. "Put any knickknacks you might not like in the closet out of your way. Rearrange the room however you want. Just make yourself to home—completely. This is your sanctuary, your escape valve when life in a big family gets to be too much for you."

Mom Wynters opened a door, revealing the bathroom between Kari's and Mindy's room. "The boys' rooms are on the other side of the stairwell. Dad and I are at the back of the house." The woman pushed a stray lock of Kari's thick, black hair into place and again stated how happy she was to have Kari there for the summer.

The young woman blinked back the tears blurring her eyes. "Thanks. Everything's perfect. Thanks," she hesitated, then gulped, "Mom."

"Mom." How strange the word sounded to Kari's ears. Sheena, her real mother, hated to be reminded that she was old enough to have a mature daughter. She hadn't allowed Kari to call her "mother" since Kari entered first grade. It wasn't until tonight, amid all this love, that Kari realized just how much she'd missed it.

Mom Wynters paused and straightened the delicately crocheted doily on the bureau. "I think you should know that my sister, Amanda, didn't tell us about any problems you might be facing. She did say, however, that you accepted Jesus as your Saviour last year and that she'd miss your company terribly."

Kari studied the woman's animated face. "Just remember," Mom continued, "that should you want to talk, should you need to talk, I'm here." After another hug and a kiss, the gently rounded woman left, leaving Kari to get accustomed to her unfamiliar surroundings.

"I never imagined I'd be sleeping in a storybook bedroom like this," Kari thought as she dropped her largest suitcase onto the white comforter. She ran her hand across the French-provincial bedstead and along the ruffle on the arched canopy. The frilly, white embroidered curtains fluttered lightly in the breeze coming through the two partially opened windows.

Kari kicked off her high heels and twirled about, hugging herself in delight. The memory of her home in Chicago, of her mother's walk-up apartment, the tiny cubicle of a bedroom, hardly large enough for a single bed and a dresser, the faded wallpaper and the cluttered parlor strewn with wine bottles flashed through her mind. She frowned at the final scene, the freakish drama she'd been forced to endure.

For the hundredth time Sheena's hate-filled eyes flashed through Kari's mind. Every tormenting word, every gesture of ugliness replayed in her thoughts. She pressed her hands over her ears to blot out the memory, but nothing eased her pain. It seemed as though the scenes in her imagination had happened just yesterday.

"How dare you!" Sheena had spat out her venom. "In my own house, my daughter, and my husband! And you, young lady, pretending to be a Christian! Get out! Get out of my house and never come back!"

"No, Sheena, no! Please! It wasn't like that. Keith forced his way into my bedroom and tried to seduce me. When I refused, he got angry and then tried to— to— to—" Kari couldn't continue. She had clutched her torn sleeve about her arm as if hiding the rent garment would make the horrible nightmare go away.

Sheena's fury turned on Keith. "You— you—"

"Your little tramp of a daughter has been throwing herself at me for months," Keith had drawled. "I'm surprised you haven't noticed." His entire demeanor oozed of self-assurance.

A look of uncertainty flashed across Sheena's mottled face. Suddenly, she stormed into the kitchen. "I need a drink!"

Kari turned and ran to her room. Instantly, she sensed she was not alone. She turned to see Keith, standing in the doorway, leering. "You don't really believe that your mother will side with you over me," he taunted. "She loves me. And whether she believes you or not, I'll win in the long-run. Get that through your stupid head. And you'd better beware, little Miss Prude. Sooner or later—"

Kari longed to believe Keith wrong. But deep inside the practical Kari, the Kari that videotaped all the pain inflicted during the years of drunken tirades, the embarrassment of having an alcoholic for a mother, the abuse and neglect delivered by one "father" after another, admitted to herself that Keith was right. Kari also knew that next time Sheena might not be there to save her, and Keith would carry out his threat.

Kari had relived the scene so many times since that night. "If only Sheena had opposed my leaving. If only she'd assured me of her love. If only she believed me. If only—" Kari shook her head violently, fighting to destroy the image that haunted her peace of mind. Forcing her mind back to the present, she grabbed a handful of clothes from her suitcase and placed them in the top drawer of the dresser.

Strange creaks and groans filled the night air as the old farmhouse settled for the night. Kari wasn't sure just how long she stood staring out at the moonlit world beyond her window. The tranquil scene calmed her spirit. She thought of Marc, of Dad Wynters, and of Michael. How different from Keith they seemed.

"But one can't always trust appearances," Kari argued silently.

When the gong from the old miller's clock in the hallway announced 1:00 a.m., Kari yawned and picked up her Bible from the nightstand.

"Lo, I am with you always, even unto the ends of the earth." From Kari's big-town perspective, a sprawling dairy farm fifteen miles outside of Beaver Dam, Wisconsin, fit that description all too well.

She snuggled beneath the covers and switched off the light. Though she tried to recall her eventful day, the uninterrupted darkness of the starry night and the downy-soft mattress engulfed her. She felt exhausted, almost too tired to sleep. Kari tried to dredge up memories of her day, to relive the tearful farewell with Amanda and the children, her last view of Chicago's skyline, the dirty towns and noisy cities she'd passed through. And meeting Marc. The diner. Marc. The velvet night sky. Marc, and again, Marc.

"Stop it!" She moaned. "You don't have time for romances and dreams that go poof with the dawn, remember? When you're tempted, just think of Keith, your mother's ever-loving husband. That thought should keep you from making a fool out of yourself over Marc, or any other male, for that matter." Kari closed her eyes again.

Strange, disjointed scenes pulsated before her eyes, interwoven with the faces of Keith, then Marc, then Keith again. She pictured Marc helping her from the truck. Except when she smiled down at him, Marc's grin dissolved into Keith's leering sneer.

"No! Go away! Let go of me! Keith, leave me alone! I'll tell my mother if you come any closer!" Kari screamed, crying, trembling uncontrollably. She fumbled for the switch on the lamp beside her bed. "Where is that thing, anyway?" Without warning, the bedroom door burst open. Kari screamed again and pulled the covers to her neck.

The hall light flooded the room. "Kari, what's wrong? Are you all right?" Mom Wynters, wrapped in a furry, pink robe, rushed to the bed and reached for the sobbing girl.

"What happened? Did someone break into the house?" Sleepy-eyed Michael and a frightened Mindy peeked through the door. Marc and his dad moved to the foot of the bed, poised to do battle with an invisible foe.

"Everyone go back to bed. It's OK. The poor girl had a nightmare, that's all. She doesn't need an audience." Mom sat on the bed beside Kari. "You just woke up in a strange place, Honey, and it frightened you, that's all. You'll be fine," Mom soothed. She turned to the rest of the family. "Go on now, all of you. You still have three more hours of sleep before milking time."

The mention of five o'clock chores caused the other family members to head back to their rooms. Mom held Kari in her arms, rocking the sobbing girl back and forth as she would a five-year-old.

"I'm sorry I woke everyone up. I'm so embarrassed. Did I say anything?" Kari's words caught in the middle of a hiccup.

"I don't know. We thought someone had tried to break into the house." Mom Wynters chuckled. "Did you see that baseball bat that Marc grabbed? I'd feel sorry for anyone who tried to break into our house with Marc and his dad around. Just relax. Here, you climb back under the covers and let me get you a drink of water."

Kari watched through swollen eyelids as the woman stepped from the room, then returned with a glass of water. The cool, refreshing well water did help Kari to regain her composure.

"Now, try to sleep. Would you feel better if I stayed awhile?" The woman placed the half-empty tumbler on the night stand. "I'll leave this here in case you get thirsty in the night."

"Thank you, I'll be fine. I truly will." Kari nestled further under the quilt, her eyes dark with apprehension. "A light might help though."

Mom Wynters patted the girl's arm. "OK, I'll leave the desk lamp on. Don't be afraid to call me if you need me. I'm right down the hall. You should sleep in tomorrow morning. You've plenty of time to get accustomed to our unearthly hours." Kari nodded sleepily.

"Poor little girl," Mom Wynters continued, "It's been a rough day, leaving your home and everything that's familiar behind, to risk living with total strangers for three months."

Waves of sleep washed over Kari, making her barely aware of the woman kneeling beside her bed. "Something's bothering the child, Lord. Give her peace so she can rest tonight, Father. I feel so helpless."

# Chapter 4
# Learning to Drive

Kari splashed her face with cold water in order to wake up. Unaccustomed to the early morning hours, she decided that fitting into the Wynters' family schedule proved more difficult than fitting into the Wynters family. She had babysat Amanda's two children, Megan and Sammy, nights while Amanda worked at the agency, and attended classes at the hospital during the day, so at first Kari found it difficult to restructure her sleep patterns.

Each morning there were pancakes to flip, eggs to scramble, grapefruit to section, a table to set, and hungry farmers to feed. And each morning, Dad Wynters, Marc, and Michael returned to the house ravenous, having already milked the 65-head herd.

The first morning that Kari watched the family eat she stared, mesmerized. She'd never seen anyone eat so much, so early in the day. She felt queasy at the sight. No matter how many flapjacks Mom Wynters stacked on the platter, it was always empty before the plate reached the table cloth.

Mom Wynters noticed Kari's astonishment and laughed, tousling her oldest son's hair. "These men work like horses and eat like them too."

Mindy giggled. "Wait until Sunday." She warned. "We'll have waffles with homemade strawberry jam on top. Ooo-wee! Will they eat then!"

"Hey, I wouldn't talk if I were you," Michael retorted. "Meet Mindy, the human vacuum cleaner!" He pointed to Mindy's third helping of scrambled eggs.

"May I get a word in edgewise this morning?" Dad Wynters interjected before Mindy fired her reply. "Ruth, I need you to go into town to Winchell's Feed Store today. I've run out of vitamins for the calves. I can't leave old Bernie. She'll deliver anytime now."

Mom Wynters frowned. "Oh, honey, I'm sorry, but I promised Grandma Lewis that I'd take her to Madison this morning for her doctor's appointment. She's been having nagging pains around her heart. It's taken me a week just to convince her to go to a specialist. You know how she is about spending money." Suddenly Mom Wynters brightened. "Kari, do you drive?"

"I wish I did, but I'm afraid I never had any reason to learn while living in Chicago. The El [elevated railroad] runs right past our front door."

"Would you like to learn?" Mom asked, speculation gleaming in her eyes.

Kari's eyes widened with excitement. "I'd love to."

"You'll be sorry," Marc teased. "I won't, but you will. You'll become our newest gofer."

"I'll drive, Dad," Michael volunteered, trying to appear magnanimous.

Dad grinned and tapped Michael's shoulder. "Next year, Son, next year." He paused. "Well, that leaves Marc. I'd hoped he could repair the fence on the back forty today," he sighed.

Mom Wynters collected the plates and silverware from around the table. "By the way, Mindy, you're going with me. Grandma Lewis feels deprived when you don't come along." Mom Wynters talked as she cleared the table. "If Kari went to town with Marc they could stop at the Motor Vehicle Bureau for a driver's manual, and she could begin studying for her permit. You'd have nothing to do around here all day, Kari."

Kari laughed. "Nothing to do? I've never been anywhere where there's always so *much* to do," she exclaimed.

Dad Wynters opened his well-worn Bible. "We'd better get on with worship. I've got to get back to the barn and poor Bernie. She's having a rough time."

Kari listened as Dad Wynters read from Matthew 6, finishing with verse 34: "Therefore do not worry about tomorrow, for tomorrow will worry about itself. Each day has enough trouble of its own."

As she knelt with the rest of the family for prayer, Kari mulled the words of the text over in her mind. "Each day has enough trouble of its own." There was no doubt in her mind that this day would definitely have its share of troubles without worrying about the next.

When they arose from their knees, Marc started for the door, then turned to Kari. "Can you be ready in twenty minutes? I'll gas up the truck and pull it around to the front of the house."

Kari avoided his gaze. "Uh, sure. Let me finish helping Mom clean up the breakfast dishes."

But Mom Wynters had other plans. "No problem. You scoot upstairs and get ready. Mindy and I have plenty of time to finish these off."

Precisely twenty minutes later Kari heard the raspy honk of the truck horn. "Be right down!" she called out the open window. "Well, here goes," she thought, running the palm of her hands along the seams of her blue jeans. "I vowed I'd stay out of Marc's way. I don't need a man to confuse my life. But you have to admit, he's quite a man, Lord." Kari grabbed her white clutch purse, took one last look at herself in the full-length mirror, and ran down the stairs.

At the foot of the stairs, Mindy shoved a large wicker basket into Kari's arms. "Here. Mom insisted that I pack you two a lunch since Dad stuck in an extra huge list of errands for Marc to run. You'll never get them all done before suppertime. Tell Marc to take you to Wisconsin State Reserve Park for lunch. You'll love the lake." Mindy winked knowingly and added a two-quart thermos jug to Kari's load. Kari thanked the girl and hurried to the waiting truck.

The radio was blaring out one of her favorite popular songs as she hopped into the cab. Kari sighed with relief. "At least we won't ride in silence," she thought, smiling to herself.

"What's so funny?" Marc eased the truck down the tree-arched driveway onto the county road.

Kari pursed her lips. "Wouldn't you like to know," she thought, but she said, "Nothing much." She glanced out of the window at a flock of crows swooping in and out of a field of young corn that grew along her side of the roadway.

"Come on, let me in on your secret," Marc teased, a smile forming at the edge of his mouth.

Kari demured, "How far is it to Beaver Dam?"

"You're not answering my question." Marc stepped down on the accelerator. The truck leaped forward into the passing lane and around a slow-moving tractor hauling a wagon.

Kari frowned. "Is Gradma Lewis related on your mother's side of the family or your dad's?"

"Neither. She's no blood relation at all," Marc replied. "But she's been a member of the family ever since Mom and Dad purchased the farm as newlyweds."

"Well, I am a licensed nurse, though not in Wisconsin. I would be glad to look in on her occasionally if it would help."

Marc glanced over at Kari and smiled. "I know my mom would appreciate that. She's quite a lady, you know, my Grandma Lewis. Did you know that she and her family came to Wisconsin in an old farm wagon pulled by two horses when she was five years old? Wait until she regales you with the story of the crossing!"

"Sounds fascinating."

"It is." Marc and Kari rode in silence for more than ten minutes. Kari's face brightened when they reached the edge of the town. "People! Automobiles! I don't believe it. Civilization!"

"Humph! Too crowded for my blood," Marc growled.

Kari ignored his peeve. "Well, what's the schedule?" she asked.

"You know," Marc suggested as he stopped for a traffic light, "if we picked up your driver's manual first thing, you could study it while I fill Dad's shopping list, and you'd be ready to get your permit before we leave town today."

"Hey, wait! I doubt that very much," Kari started. "You must understand that I have never even—"

"Sure you could. I can review you while we eat lunch. Then you'll go in and pass the test. I might even let you drive home if you're good," Marc teased.

"You're crazy, do you know that? I've never driven anything larger than a bicycle in my entire life." Kari shook her head, staring incredulously at Marc's composure. For him, the discussion was over.

"You're serious, aren't you?"

An emphatic nod assured her that he was indeed serious. "Dad needs another driver on the farm badly. There are times that Mom and I can't drop everything and go. And since we're here in town, why not save a trip? Besides, when I leave for college in the fall, Mom will be stuck doing all the driving."

"Hey, I'm only supposed to be here for the summer, remember?" Kari reminded. Somehow the thought of leaving the Wynter's home made her stomach lurch.

Ignoring her remark, he continued. "Yep, it sure would be a help to the family. Mindy will be resuming piano lessons soon, and her gymnastics class. Then there are 4-H meetings for both Michael and Mindy and football practices for Michael. Yep, sure would be a big help."

"OK, OK, OK! I'll try," Kari muttered. "How many times does the state allow you to flunk?"

"The state? Three, I think. Me? None!" Marc said as the truck jerked forward in the traffic.

All too soon for Kari, Marc stopped in front of a large, imposing, red-brick building. The sign read "Department of Motor Vehicles." "Oh," Kari thought "what have I gotten myself into this time?"

They hurried inside the building, located a driver's manual, and left. At first the manual with its confusing diagrams and directions appeared to Kari's ignorant eyes to be written in Swahili. Nothing made any sense, but she persisted.

Hours later, after numerous stops and views of crowded parking lots, grain stores, machine shops, and hardware stores, Marc jumped back into the driver's seat and announced, "I'm hungry! Those pancakes didn't stick any too long, did they? Where would you like to go to eat lunch?"

"I don't know. You know this town better than I do." Kari barely lifted her face from the driver's manual.

"Would you like to go over to the State Reserve? You'll like it. The folks used to pack a picnic lunch on hot summer days, and we'd go over there to feed the ducks after church."

Kari looked up momentarily. "I think Mindy mentioned something about the State Reserve."

Marc maneuvered the truck through the busy streets to the edge of town. Minutes later the truck stopped. Kari continued studying the different road signs while Marc hopped out of the cab, grabbed the lunch basket from the back, and rounded the truck. "Hi, my name's Marc. What's yours?" He shouted into Kari's half-opened window.

Kari jumped. "Oh, I'm sorry. But you *did* tell me to study."

"Well, I take it all back." Marc lifted his eyebrows in mock despair as he opened her door.

"Do you mean that I don't have to take the test today?" Kari reached for her purse.

"No, it does not, young lady," Marc replied, leading her down the sloped lawn toward the lake. "How's this spot, here under the tree? We could drive farther into the park if you'd like. Or there are picnic tables in that grove of trees over there." He pointed across the lake.

"No, this is fine, more like a picnic somehow." Kari tucked the manual into her purse.

Marc set the lunch basket on the lawn, then sprinted toward the pickup. "I think Michael left his sleeping bag behind the seat last week after the church campout. We can sit on that." A moment later he returned with the bag. He unzipped it and smoothed it out under the tree. Kari spread a green-and-white-checkered table cloth over the bag, all the while listening to Marc as he shared his memories of the park.

"One time when I was around five years old I got so enthusiastic skipping stones that I walked right into the lake after a particularly flat one. I ruined my best pair of shoes. They shrank." Marc laughed as he opened the basket and began placing the plastic covered dishes on the table cloth. The sandwiches, the carrot and celery sticks, and the chocolate cake disappeared almost as fast as had the morning pancakes. Feeling comfortably full and relaxed, Marc unbuttoned the neck of his plaid shirt and stretched out in the sun. "When I wake up, I'll quiz you on the book," he yawned, "so be prepared!"

"Tyrant!" Kari teased.

The sultry afternoon sun shining through the leaves of the tree formed lacy patterns on the dull brown sleeping bag. Kari leaned her back against the tree and tried to concentrate on the small type in the book before her. She glanced over at Marc. She smiled thinking how much he resembled a small boy when his face was relaxed. "Could he really be as guileless as he appears, or is he a good actor?" she wondered.

The whispering breeze lulled her into a half-conscious state. The book fell to her lap. Her head tipped to one side, and her lips parted slightly.

A fly, arriving too late for lunch, decided to explore the prospects of a meal on Marc's arm. Marc swatted at it, but the insect persisted.

"Forget it!" Marc groaned. "Let's have a look at that driver's manual." He raised up on one elbow and looked over at Kari sleeping against the tree trunk.

Intending to carry the picnic basket back to the truck, Marc got to his feet and circled the tree. For a moment he stood silently watching her. He smiled at the childlike peace on her relaxed face. He knelt beside her.

"You are so beautiful," he murmured, reaching out to push a stray, ebony curl from her cheek.

Startled, Kari's eyes flashed open. Her lips tensed when she saw Marc's face at such close range.

"Wha—" she began.

"Sssh! It's OK. I didn't mean to waken you. But we've got to get going if we plan to make it to the DMV before they close for the day." Taking her arms, he drew her to her feet and paused. She could read a momentary confusion in his eyes. He leaned slowly forward, but Kari pulled away and bent to retrieve the empty picnic basket.

"Please Marc, let's keep things simple. Remember, at the end of the summer I'll go home to Chicago, and you'll go back to the university."

"I know. I promised myself that I wouldn't get involved with any home-town girls this summer. I'm determined to leave Wisconsin unchained." He scooped up the sleeping bag and shook it.

"Great! Then we are—just friends," Kari said.

Kari hurried up the hill to the truck, anxious to escape the tension. "That *is* the way I want it too!" she argued with herself as she set the basket in the truck bed.

Pasting an enthusiastic smile on her face she whirled to face Marc. "We'd better get over to that Motor Vehicle Bureau so I can take that test, huh?"

Marc dug the toe of his boot into the loose sand beside the truck, momentarily ignoring her question. "Huh? Oh, yes, we'd better hurry."

As the truck roared from the park, Mark snapped on the radio, raising the volume to a level that prevented conversation.

"Fine," Kari thought. The last thing she wanted was to discuss the turmoil she felt inside. Determined more than ever to pass the test for her driver's permit, she pushed thoughts of idyllic picnics and hand-some farm boys aside and concentrated on parking regulations, speed limits, and safe braking distances.

By four fifteen, when Marc finally parked the pickup truck in front of the Department of Motor Vehicles, Kari's head ached from her intense concentration. Marc gazed at the red-brick building for a few moments, then turned toward her. "Hey, sorry about being so—"

Nervously, she pushed the truck door open. "No problem. It's no big deal. I'm not ready for a relationship right now either."

"No," he hastened, fumbling for the right words. "I didn't mean about that. I just wanted to apologize for being so bossy before, about the test, I mean. It's OK if you don't pass it today."

Kari's face reddened, and her eyes avoided his. "Oh, yeah, sure. Thanks. Well, here goes. Wish me luck." She shot from the truck and into the building, embarrassed that she'd misunderstood.

Fifteen minutes later Kari burst from the building, waving a yellow sheet of paper. "I did it!" She squealed, skipping and twirling as she approached the truck. Marc stood by her open door and helped her into the cab with the flourish of a cavalier.

"If you'd like to drive home?" Marc began.

She waved his suggestion aside. "Oh, no. Just getting this thing is enough excitement for one day."

For the first ten minutes Kari talked nonstop about the test, but an awkward silence developed after she'd exhausted that subject. She felt tempted to turn on the radio again. Instead, she leaned back against the seat and closed her eyes. "Ah, I do wish this headache would go away."

Marc murmured an appropriate reply and concentrated on the empty highway before him.

# Chapter 5
# Friends at the River

Mom Wynters beamed with pride when she learned that Kari got her permit on the first try. "The men in this family are too impatient for such things," she confided. "We'll go driving tomorrow morning. I'll teach you the right way."

During the weeks that followed, Kari and Mom Wynters spent an hour each day driving. That hour became Kari's favorite time of day. She enjoyed listening to Mom Wynters share family anecdotes about the children growing up, and occasionally she relaxed enough to reveal parts of her own childhood.

"Sheena, my mother that is, can't really help the way she is. I hated her for a long time. But your sister helped me to accept my mother's limitations. There are times still when I watch the way you and Dad Wynters deal with Mindy, and I wish—Oh well, as Sheena always said, 'If wishes were horses, beggars would ride.' "

Mom Wynters glanced over at Kari. "Honey, Dad and I are far from perfect. The only strength we have is from the good Lord. We don't have any powers that you can't have too, regardless of your less-than-ideal childhood. Just give God time. He knows your heart and knows what is best for you. Look how He brought you to Amanda, then to us."

By the end of June, Kari had passed her regular driver's test. Marc's prediction proved correct. Suddenly her driving skills were in great demand. Between playing chauffeur to Michael and Mindy and running the normal farm errands, she became quite adept at driving.

Since the day in the park, Kari found it convenient to avoid Marc. With so many rooms in the remodeled farmhouse, she managed to be somewhere else whenever he arrived home.

The month of July kept the family busier than ever. The weeds in the garden dared Kari and Mindy to keep up with them, though the rich, black soil guaranteed an abundant harvest almost without the weeding.

Kari felt awed by the miracle of growth every time she picked tomatoes or tossed a salad of home-grown lettuce or snapped green beans for freezing.

Late one afternoon Mom Wynters and Kari were out behind the house picking the last row of ripe bush beans. Mindy was spending the afternoon at her best friend's house making decorations for a teen party. Mom Wynters grabbed her bucket by the handle, straightened up and stretched, and gasped. "Ooh! That hurts! A stitch in my back." She dropped the bucket and put her hand on her lower back.

Kari noted the pain on the woman's face and reached to help. "You need a good back rub, Mom. I'll finish this row of beans and go start the potatoes for supper while you take a shower. Then I'll give you the best back rub of your life." Kari laughed, wiping the sweat from her brow.

"I think I'll take you up on your offer," Mom grunted. "I don't know what I did, but my back really hurts." She limped painfully toward the kitchen door.

"I'll be right in. Just relax on your bed if you're ready before I get there." Kari hurried along the row, snapping off the crisp, ripe beans. Returning to the house, she dumped the beans into the kitchen sink and covered them with cold water, then washed several potatoes and put them in the oven to bake. Going upstairs, she grabbed a tall bottle of pink hand lotion from the counter in the bathroom and hurried to Mom Wynter's room. She paused at the bedroom door. "Are you ready?"

"I certainly am. I appreciate this," Mom Wynters said, turning onto her stomach. "When Shelly was home, she used to give me back rubs from time to time. Mindy is too impatient. She tires within a few minutes." She rested her head on her arms and let Kari's smooth, gentle hands ease out the knots along her spine.

Kari smiled. She couldn't believe how much this kind, gentle woman had become more of a mother to her than her own mother ever had been. For that matter, the whole family felt like the family she'd never known. That is, except for Marc. "He'll never be a brother," she thought, shaking her head.

"I really enjoy having you here, Kari. I'm not going to want to let you go at the end of the summer. You've been a big help," Mom sighed.

"I'm not going to want to go," Kari admitted. "I've never felt more at home anywhere."

Mom rested her head on her folded hands as Kari's expert fingers kneaded the woman's shoulders. "Really? Sometimes I get the impression that Marc makes you uncomfortable. He hasn't annoyed you in any way, has he?"

"Annoyed me?" Kari thought. "Hardly annoy. More like confuse, or weaken my resolve perhaps." Suddenly sensing that Mom was waiting for a reply, she answered. "No, of course not. Marc has been quite a gentleman around me."

"I'm glad. We've tried to impress upon our boys the importance of treating girls respectfully. It pleases me to know that he hasn't let us down." The woman's shoulders relaxed further.

"Everyone has been very kind to me. I am afraid, however, that Michael is developing sort of a crush on me," Kari confessed.

"I've noticed. That's typical of a fifteen-year-old, I guess. He'll be fine when school starts and he's back in the classroom around girls his own age," Mom assured her.

The sound of an approaching tractor sent Kari to the window. "Oh dear, it's the men. I'd better run down to the kitchen and check the potatoes. You stay here. I can take care of supper. Do you feel a little better?"

"Yes. Are you sure you can manage?" Mom Wynters gathered her cotton lounging robe about her shoulders.

Kari skipped down the stairs. "Of course, I can. I learned from a pro!" She called back.

Mindy had arrived home by the time the men finished showering. The delicious aromas of freshly baked potato boats with sour cream, king-size burgers, and tossed salad raised the spirits of the entire family. The strawberry-rhubarb pie a la mode topped off a perfect meal, except for the subdued atmosphere caused by Mom's absence. Dad pushed himself from the table. "I'm going up to see if Mother is feeling any better."

"Anyone for a swim at the river?" Marc suggested as he helped carry the last of the dinner dishes to the sink. Michael and Mindy shouted and ran for their swim suits.

"How about you, Kari?"

Kari longed for a cool dip before bedtime. "Will your dad be going?"

"Naw," Dad answered from the doorway, "Mom's sleeping. We old folks will stay here tonight. You go, Kari. I'm going into the den and work on the books."

"Hurry up. We don't have all night," Marc laughed.

Reluctantly Kari climbed the stairs and slipped into her emerald green bathing suit. She eyed herself thoughtfully in the full-length wall mirror and felt comfortable with what she saw. "Not spectacular, but you'll do, Kari Gerard," she decided. At the sound of the horn, she grabbed a towel and ran down to the waiting truck.

"I'll ride in the back with Mindy and Michael." She skipped past the open door of the cab and hopped into the truck bed beside Mindy.

"Marc wanted you to ride in the cab with him," Mindy whispered.

"What? What did you say? I can't hear you. All this wind, you know." Kari leaned over the edge and let the breeze blow in her face. "This feels great after a day in the garden."

Michael and Mindy jumped from the truck before it came to a full stop and raced for the river. The cool refreshing current massaged Kari's stiff muscles. Shrieks of delight filled the little clearing as they played tag and took turns dunking one other. The sun disappeared behind the trees, casting long, deep shadows on the water's surface.

Having been dunked far more than her share, Kari grinned devilishly at Marc, who stood with his back to her, watching Mindy and Michael wrestle near the shore. Hardly making a ripple in the water's surface, she dived into the water, swam up behind him, and knocked his legs out from under him. He sank with a loud yell and splash, then surfaced, gasping for air.

"Why, you little sneak!" He lunged toward her swiftly retreating figure. "I'll get you for that one."

Swimming faster than she'd ever swum before, Kari headed downstream. She heard Marc behind her as she rounded the first bend of the river. Taking a deep breath she dived again, only to be dragged back up to the surface, face to face with Marc.

"Thought you could outswim me, did you? Get ready to be dunked," he warned, tightly grasping her left upper arm and the top of her head. "One, two, three." She fought as he pushed her beneath the water, then hauled her back to the surface. "Here you go again. I always pay two for one."

Kari started to protest, only to be met by a large gulp of water.

"Are you sorry? No? I guess you haven't learned your lesson yet." He held her at arm's length, at his height, before he sent her below for the third time. As they stared at one another, Kari recognized the same look of confusion that had filled his eyes once before, at the park.

"You're irresistible, do you know that?" He paused. She lifted her eyes to his and gave a short little shake of her head. Shouts in the distance broke the spell.

"Hey, you two! Where have you been?" Michael shouted as Kari and Marc returned upstream.

"Don't ask, stupid!" Mindy hissed at her brother.

"Ride in the cab with me?" Marc lifted one eyebrow and grinned a crooked, dimpled grin.

"It *is* getting a bit chilly out." Kari hoped Mindy and Michael would take her excuse at face value.

As they bounced over the field, back to the farm road, Marc reached across the seat and placed his large, rough hand over hers. She edged her hand away.

"Are you afraid of me?" Marc asked incredulously, glancing at Kari out of the corner of his eye.

"No, of course not. I'm just cold," Kari snapped.

"I hope not," Marc said, swinging the truck on the main road toward the farmhouse. Several minutes later he turned the truck up the long driveway to the house, then screeched to a stop.

"What's going on? You bounced us all over the truck bed," Mindy yelled as Marc hopped out of the pickup.

"Nothing, absolutely nothing!" Marc sauntered off toward the barn. "I have some chores to finish!"

"Yikes! What's with him?" Mindy asked Kari as they climbed the porch steps.

"Sssh! Mom and Dad are already asleep." Kari hurried up the stairs.

"But, I thought—" Mindy followed her to her room.

"What did you think, Mindy?" Kari snapped.

"Well, I, uh—" Tears welled up in Mindy's eyes, and her lip quivered threateningly.

"I'm sorry for snapping at you, Mindy. I didn't mean to. It's just that Marc and I don't seem to be able to get on the same wavelength, that's all."

"Michael will be glad to hear that. He wasn't too happy when he saw you and Marc kissing at the river," Mindy blurted. "Oops! I wasn't suppose to tell. I'm sorry. Please don't let Michael know I said anything."

Kari turned and looked at Mindy. "First of all, we weren't kissing. Get it in your head that Marc and I are barely friends," she insisted.

"Oh, yeah, OK. Good night." Mindy kissed Kari on the cheek. "I like having you as a sister, Kari."

"I like you, too, very much," Kari assured her. Mindy gave a little wave and closed her bedroom door behind her.

Kari stared at her reflection in the dressing table mirror for a long moment. "No guys, remember? No guys!"

After a quick shower, Kari threw back the bedcovers, pulled the sheet up around her shoulders, and tried to fall asleep.

As the comforting darkness settled about her, Marc's face swam before her eyes intermittently with Keith's. "Oh no, not again!" She shook herself awake. "I won't dream that horrid dream again."

She snapped on the lamp beside her bed. "Maybe I can read for a while," she thought. "Some of Mom's chocolate-chip cookies and milk would surely taste good right now."

Slipping into her satin robe, she tiptoed down the stairs, through the parlor, and into the dining room. As she felt along the wall for the light switch, a large hand closed over hers.

"Sssh, don't scream. It's only me," a voice whispered in her ear. Kari gasped in surprise.

"What are you doing down here, Michael?" she whispered.

"The same thing you are, probably. I'm hungry." He turned on the kitchen light.

Kari laughed. "Guilty! All I could think about was Mom's chocolate-chip cookies. I'll get the milk and you get the cookie jar," she suggested.

"Yes, ma'am!" Michael reached for a giant ceramic teddy bear jar. For a time they ate in silence. "You know, this is the first time we've been together without Marc around." Michael dipped another cookie in his glass.

Kari acted nonchalant. "Really? I hadn't noticed."

"No, I suppose not. I've had enough. I'm going up to bed." Michael scooped up his glass and his plate and rinsed them in the sink before placing them in the dishwasher. "Good night."

"Good night, Michael. Sleep well." Kari began cleaning up the crumbs scattered across the kitchen bar. Carefully she replaced the cookie jar and rinsed out the dish cloth.

She turned in time to see Marc leaning against the doorjamb watching her. "Michael. Isn't he a little young for you?"

"I beg your pardon?" Her face flushed, and anger darted from her eyes. "No, don't answer that. I'll pretend I didn't hear you."

"You're right; I'm sorry. Friends again?" Marc grinned sheepishly.

Kari nodded. "Friends again. Now if you'll excuse me, I'm going upstairs to my room."

Weeks passed. Kari and Marc alternated between clumsy attempts at communication and speaking only when silence proved embarrassing. She watched the many ways Marc displayed respect for his mother and father. She noted his teasing, yet tender banter with Mindy. She observed his good moods and his bad. The fact that he didn't fit the image of men that she'd constructed in her mind frustrated her. She could see how much Marc resembled his father. He was not at all like Keith, even when angry. Confusion filled her heart.

While she and Mom Wynters worked side by side each day, they talked of many things, but never of Marc. She wished she could discuss her feelings about Marc with Mom. But as yet, Kari felt too uncertain herself how she actually felt.

Kari's weekly visits to Grandma Lewis's place supplied a change of pace, but failed to ease the confusion. Though she never sat down and actually told the woman, "I have a problem," Grandma Lewis always seemed to sense when something was wrong. It was unnerving to Kari. Gradma had a way of surmising, taking aim, and hitting the target without ever being told the problem.

Even though Marc's name seldom came up in their conversation, Kari knew without a doubt that Grandma understood. She also knew that Grandma suspicioned Kari's animosity toward men in general, and that she understood that it was related to her life before coming to Wisconsin.

"Kari, you need to let go," she said one day. "The past is the past, and your future is in God's hands. That just leaves today to worry about."

For days after, Grandma's words tumbled through her mind wherever she went. As she rinsed dishes, as she weeded the flower gardens, as she helped with the laundry, Kari remembered—"Just for today."

Each night when she knelt beside her bed, Kari asked God to help her let go, to teach her how to trust people again. She longed to believe that all men weren't the same, that Marc wasn't like Keith. Yet somehow the fear wedged deep in her heart refused to go away.

And each morning when she looked at the small business calendar on the desk beside her bed she mourned the quickly fading summer.

# Chapter 6
# Narrow Escape

Kari stood before the kitchen sink, methodically rinsing the breakfast dishes and placing them in the dishwasher. An unaccustomed silence pervaded the farmhouse. Mom had left right after breakfast to take Mindy to the dentist. Earlier, Dad, Michael, and Marc had left for the hay fields immediately after they heard the morning weather forecast. Severe thunder storms were moving in, with possible tornado conditions. The second crop of hay for the season would be ruined if they didn't get it harvested before the storm.

Kari stood for a time looking out on the vegetable garden and noted that another crop of plump orange tomatoes had colored to a bright red. Squash vines threatened to overrun the melon patch. With the last dish loaded in the washer, she ran the dishcloth over the stove top and the counters.

"I'd better start the family wash," she mused. "I need to boil eggs for the men's lunch." The sun shone through the white dotted swiss café curtains and sparkled across the chrome faucet. "Hm, no rain clouds yet. It's still a great day for a picnic."

Kari bustled from room to room, vacuuming, dusting, changing the linen, and watering plants. "One more room," Kari thought. "Marc's." The clock at the base of the stairs gonged eleven times as she folded and tucked in the last corner on Marc's top sheet. "The earth tones fit his personality," she said to herself. Smoothing the beige-and-navy comforter under the matching pillows, Kari felt comfortably domestic, almost as though she were playing house. She opened the window beside the bed to let in the fresh morning air.

Track and field ribbons along with various other high-school awards decorated the bulletin board over his desk. Dogeared copies of *Tom Sawyer and Huckleberry Finn*, *Treasure Island*, *The Voyage of the Kon-Tiki*, and *The Complete Works of Ray Bradbury* lined the top shelf of the bookcase, along with all of James Herriot's series of veterinary books.

Kari picked up a well-marked copy of *The Sermons of Peter Marshall* that lay open, face down, on the nightstand beside the bed. She idly scanned the chapter he must have been reading. "Interesting," she thought. "You can learn a lot about a person by what he reads." She smiled to herself. "Does this knight's armor ever need buffing?" she wondered.

While examining each of his awards and ribbons, she tried to picture him as he must have looked while in grade school—freckle faced with hair plastered to his forehead, proudly accepting his blue ribbons for running and high jumping. In her mind, she followed him through high school, moving year by year from white to red to blue ribbons. With very little effort she could visualize teenage girls falling all over themselves to make certain he noticed them. Knowing the stringent requirements demanded of veterinary students, she wondered how he found time to be on the university track and field team.

The gong on the hall clock struck twelve, jarring Kari back to reality. She reminded herself that Marc definitely was not perfect, that he could be domineering and overbearing, that occasionally he forgot things, that he was still a man, and therefore dangerous. She convinced herself that though he appeared to be very different from Keith, he was certain to eventually hurt her somehow. "Real life just isn't like that," she muttered. "No cotton-candy dreams for me, no vine-covered cottages, no fairy-tale endings."

Kari replaced the book on the stand, and with a heavy sigh hurried downstairs to the kitchen.

Glancing out the window, Kari was startled to see that dark, threatening clouds filled the western sky. Quickly she packed the food in the large wicker picnic basket and ran down the back steps to the driveway. She dropped the basket into the truck bed and climbed into the cab.

She pumped the accelerator. "Aw, come on. Don't hassle me now! Come on, baby. You can do it. The men are hungry. I've got to get this food to them right away." Slowly, grudgingly, the tired old engine growled and hissed to life.

Dust from the rutted farm road blew into the cab and coated Kari's clothes and face. Every other pothole bounced her clear off the driver's seat, causing her to land with a teeth shattering crash, only to be thrown into the air again. Her ponytail bobbed in erratic syncopation. Far in the distance Kari could see the dust devils surrounding the tractor and the hay wagon. Chugging to a halt by the grove of trees along the river bank she beeped the horn, announcing her arrival. She scanned the field for a glimpse of Marc. She finally spotted him heaving bales onto the wagon.

"Food!" She yelled and waved, hopping from the cab of the truck.

Leaving the farm truck and the tractor in the field Dad, Marc, and Michael ran toward her. She chose a shaded spot on the mossy bank beside the river and smoothed out the picnic blanket and table cloth.

"Wow, you're turning into some cook!" Michael exclaimed as he dropped down beside her. "Everything looks delicious."

"Thank you, kind Sir. Don't wait, just say your own blessing and eat."

Kari took a paper cup from the picnic basket and walked over to the river. Though they were upstream from the swimming hole, it was the first time she'd been back since their evening swim. She bent down and doused her dirt-streaked face with water. "Ooh, it feels so good," she murmured. Filling the paper cup with water, she poured it over her arms and hands.

"Good idea. Mind sharing the beach?" Marc laughed.

"What beach?" Kari looked startled. She hadn't heard him come up behind her.

"The one you're standing on, of course." Marc, having just removed his work boots and socks, crouched beside her and scooped up a handful of water, splashing it over his neck and face. His deep bronze tan glistened with water droplets.

"Here, let me help," Kari giggled, dumping a cup of cold water down Marc's back.

"Yeow!" Marc jumped up and grabbed the startled girl, lifting her into his arms like a sack of feed. "Let *me* help *you*!"

"Put me down! Put me down this instant!" Kari screamed.

Wading out into the stream, Marc grinned triumphantly. "*Yes Ma'am*! Whatever you say."

"Da-a-d!" Kari wailed as she felt herself falling toward the water.

Instead of surfacing, as he expected, she dived for his legs, pulling him under too. The two surfaced seconds later, sputtering and laughing.

"Hey, Michael and I will have this great lunch eaten before you two get any if you don't hurry," Dad called from the bank.

"I'm drenched!" Kari gasped, looking down at her cutoffs and blouse. "Thanks for all the help, you guys." She shook her dripping ponytail over Michael's back.

"Don't shake the water on me," Michael warned. "You asked for it."

"Well, the way I figure it, if I'm wet, everyone else should be too," she giggled, wringing out her shirtail above his head.

"Sorry to break this up, kids. We'd better finish eating and get back to work," Dad said. "We still need to complete two more times around the field before that storm hits. If I didn't know better, I'd say there's a tornado in those clouds." Dad glanced anxiously toward the rapidly approaching thunder-heads that were already beginning to shroud the hot August sun.

While the men finished eating, Kari hastened to repack the basket and tossed it onto the truck seat.

"Kari, maybe you shouldn't drive home," Dad suggested.

"I have to. I left the bedroom windows open. Everything will be soaked." Kari jumped into the cab next to the basket.

"Well, OK, but get going. You don't have much time."

Nervous because of Dad's warning, Kari drove as fast as she dared, disregarding road bumps, ruts, and scattering jack rabbits. On every curve west, Kari panicked at the rapidly changing sky. A green hue hovered over the landscape, and sharp gusts of wind blew dust off the fields and across the road in front of her. "If only I can make it back to the house. The furniture will be ruined if I don't," she chided herself. "Oh, Lord, please help me," she whispered as the truck bounced over an extra-large pothole.

Glancing into the rear-view mirror, she saw the farm truck racing toward her, followed by a whirlwind of dust. "I wonder what happened?" She pulled to the side of the dirt road and waited for it to catch up. A dust devil swirled around her as she jumped down from the cab, hurling grit and sand into her eyes and mouth. She choked and coughed, and tears filled her eyes. Over the noise of the wind she heard the farm truck screech to a stop behind her. Gravel whipped up by the tempest stung her cheeks.

Without warning, strong arms picked her up and thrust her, face down, into the drainage ditch beside the road. Her knees stung from the razor-sharp gravel and sun-baked clods of dirt along the edges of the ditch and the mud in the bottom of the ditch filled her face and oozed around her body. Her elbows stung with bruises.

"Let me go!" she screamed. "Marc, what are you doing to me?" She struggled to get up.

Marc pushed her deeper into the mud. "Keep your head down, girl," he yelled. "A tornado's coming!" He pressed the back of her head close to his chest. "And pray!"

A fearful noise roared in the distance. The sky darkened almost to midnight, and tons of topsoil flew through the air. Kari's heart pounded. She coughed and gasped for air. Her whole body convulsed uncontrollably. The sound of a thousand locomotives shook the ground, and Kari sensed that wind the speed of a bullet blew just inches over their bodies. "Don't freak out on me now, girl!" Marc yelled into her ear, and she felt his arms tighten around her.

Over the roar of the storm Kari heard a crash. "That was the pickup," Marc yelled, pressing her body closer to the ground.

A few seconds later the tornado lifted and proceeded east on its destructive course. Marc and Kari, secluded in their roadside refuge, remained silent for a few seconds. A gentle summer rain began to fall.

"It's safe now," Marc whispered. She felt him rise to his feet. A moment later he grasped her by the elbows and lifted her to her feet. "Are you OK? Can you stand up?" he asked, holding her arms with his hands. "Are you hurt? Maybe I should carry you." He brushed the tangled hair from her mud-caked face.

"No, no. I think I'm all right." She spoke barely above a whisper. Tears mingled with the raindrops ran down her face. Marc pulled a large redprint kerchief from his hip pocket and wiped a blotch of mud from her forehead.

"He's so gentle with me," she thought.

"Are you sure you're OK?" Marc held her at arm's length and searched her face.

She nodded slowly. "You saved my life. Thank you." Her teeth chattered uncontrollably and she fought an unfamiliar, unsettling urge to nestle securely in his arms.

"Hey, we're safe. You can stop shaking now." He leaned forward and brushed his lips tenderly against her forehead.

The sound of an approaching tractor broke the spell. "Dad and Michael are coming." He released her, dusting off her arms and back. "You *are* all right, aren't you? You're acting mighty strange. You're not going to faint or anything?"

Kari looked first at her mud coated form, then at Marc's, and began to giggle. "We look like we've been mud wrestling." She brushed helplessly at the mud hardening on her clothes.

Marc hopped out of the ditch and lifted Kari to the gravel roadway. "Well, we still have the farm truck." Marc gestured toward the vehicle he'd driven. "It doesn't look like the old pickup is in too great a shape."

Kari gasped at the sight of the overturned vehicle three feet beyond the drainage ditch. She realized that the tornado had picked it up and hurled it directly over their heads as they lay in the ditch. She shuddered.

Marc leaped across the narrow ditch. "I'm just glad you weren't in it when it rolled or that it didn't land on us. It looks like our guardian angels had a workout this afternoon."

Kari smiled and nodded thoughtfully.

Michael stopped the tractor beside her and hopped down. "Are you all right?" he called. Dad jumped off the back and swept Kari into his arms, giving her a gigantic bear hug.

"The pickup truck's over there." She pointed nervously toward the overturned vehicle.

"I know, but are you OK? That's what's important. "He held her at arm's length to inspect the damage. "You have some bad scrapes on your legs. Michael, take her back to the house and get those cuts seen to while I check out the damage to the pickup with Marc."

"Sure thing." Michael helped Kari into the cab of the farm truck. For the first time since the tornado hit, Kari realized that she was indeed injured. Blood from her skinned knees trickled down her legs in rivulets. Large bruises surfaced beneath the dirt on her arms. Her shoulders and neck ached. She touched her cheek bone. It hurt. "Don't worry. I bruise easily," she assured Michael as he eyed the bruise forming under her right eye.

"I know it's not my business," Michael said as the truck lurched forward, "but Marc kissed you didn't he?" His question came like a demand.

Shocked by the usually silent boy's vehemence, Kari attempted to explain. "You're right, it's not your business. However, he saved my life." Stone faced, Michael stared straight ahead at the muddy road.

"I like you a lot, Michael. You're the little brother I never had. But that doesn't give you the right to ask such personal questions. Marc and I are friends, that's all. Our relationship is— Oh, what am I saying? We don't have a relationship!" All the tension of the last hour poured out of her. She couldn't stop crying.

Michael panicked. "I'm sorry, Kari, please stop crying. It's OK if you like Marc more than me, really."

Between sniffles, Kari gasped, "I can't stop."

Michael cleared his throat. "There's a box of tissues in the glove compartment."

"Thanks!" She sniffed again.

Michael pulled the truck in beside the kitchen door. He turned off the motor and leaned forward. His brow knitted with concern. "I'm sorry, Kari. You're right. It's not my business. Maybe I just wish it were." He looked down at the steering wheel, then back at Kari. "Do you need help treating those cuts?" he asked. "Can you make it upstairs OK? I'll get the first-aid kit from the closet."

"No, I'm fine. You just go back and help your dad." Kari limped into the house and up to her room. Painfully, she padded across the soft green carpet, entered the bathroom, and slipped out of her muddy clothes. The warm shower soothed her battered body, but failed to ease her mind. She rubbed a capful of shampoo into a lather.

"I will never leave you nor forsake you. That's what You promised, Lord. I guess the promise extends farther than I thought. Thanks for protecting us from that tornado. Thanks for everything—I think."

Giant raindrops pelted the windowpanes as Kari finished drying her hair. The roar of her hairdryer blocked out the noise the men made returning from the waterlogged hayfield.

The pounding on her bedroom door startled her. "Hey, where's my white polo shirt?" Marc called. "I left it on my desk chair."

Kari slipped a yellow gingham sundress over her head, ran her hairbrush through her hair once, and opened the bedroom door. "I stuck it in the wash this morning. It might still be in the dryer."

Marc leaned against the doorjamb and grinned down at Kari. Suddenly self-conscious, she ran her fingers through her unruly curls. "Don't worry, your hair looks great that way, definitely better than it did with the applied mud pack."

Kari grimaced, then straightened herself to her full height and ordered, in a tone worthy of a master sergeant: "Mr. Wynters, lest you failed to hear, your polo shirt is downstairs in the dryer."

"Yes, Ma'am!" Marc saluted and turned toward the stairs. "You did remember to hold the starch?"

"Get on with you!" Kari fussed, throwing her hairbrush after him. "Go make yourself decent for civilized company if you can."

# Chapter 7
# Sheena's Letter

Mom puttered about the kitchen, cleaning up after another day of canning. "Kari, would you please take a box of garden produce over to Grandma Lewis? We have so many tomatoes coming on; I don't know what we'll do with them all. We've already preserved two dozen more quarts of juice than we did last year, and Dad will be bringing home a load of peaches on Thursday. We'll have to do them right away to catch them at their peak."

Kari's thumbs and fingers ached from wielding a paring knife most of the morning. She twisted her neck to loosen the kinks that seemed determined to settle in. "Sure, no problem. Shall I get some fresh lettuce from the garden too?" By now she knew Mom's routine well.

"Good idea. I'll bag a few freshly baked rolls and a couple of packs of frozen berries too. Oh yes, Dad and I are going to a Grange potluck tonight. I don't know what the rest have decided to do, but you're welcome to join us."

"Thanks, but if it's OK with you I think I'll turn in early tonight."

"By the way, Kari. Have I told you recently how much I appreciate having you here? Dad and I have been talking and, well, we would love to have you stay on. What do you say?"

Kari stammered as she reached for the garden scissors. "Thank you for offering. I hardly know what to say."

"Say Yes. Oh, I understand that you need to think it over. Take all the time you need, dear." Mom gave Kari's shoulders a squeeze. "Now to get these groceries to Grandma's place."

The hot, merciless sun beat down on Kari's left arm as she shifted the pickup into gear and eased out of the driveway. The memory of the tornado and the overturned truck haunted Kari as she drove. "How normal everything looks," she thought. Less than a week, and hardly a trace of the storm remains.

40

By the time she reached Grandma Lewis's white clapboard cottage Kari's blue cotton blouse stuck uncomfortably to her skin. A glance at the thermometer by the front door made her groan. "Ninety-five degrees!"

"Whew," she thought, "Wisconsin summers are nothing to write home about!" For a fleeting moment, she missed Lake Michigan's cooling breezes. Kari looked around at the barren, harvested fields, the abandoned barn beyond the driveway, and the empty road that disappeared over the horizon. Following a slight riffle of the window curtain, Grandma Lewis opened the door.

"Sorry to keep you waiting, but one can't be too careful these days, what with all the crime in the world." Grandma's eyes twinkled as if enjoying her own private joke.

"That's for sure, Grandma. One can never be too careful. Mom sent over some goodies for you. She included a dozen of her famous oatmeal-raisin cookies."

"How can she stand to bake in weather like this?" Grandma fussed as she tenderly removed each item from the basket.

"Oh, Mindy made these last night." The cool of the shaded cottage refreshed the perspiring Kari.

"And how is my little Mindy?" Grandma placed an armful of ripe tomatoes in the refrigerator.

"As busy as ever. She's practicing for the 4-H bake-off at the county fair, you know. I think she'll hold her own and possibly win, the way she's going at it. Mind if I sit a spell? I hate going back out in that sun." Kari sank into her favorite platform rocker, leaned back against the headrest, and closed her eyes. "So how have you been feeling?"

"I've been walking a little every day as the doctor ordered. And I'm trying to eat right, thanks to you and the Wynters. Who knows? I might outlive you all." The old woman's face crinkled into a grin as she filled two tumblers with freshly squeezed lemonade and ice. The glasses frosted instantly. "But how are you? You look tired today."

"Just the heat, I suppose." Kari took a deep breath and continued rocking.

"How's Marc?" Grandma handed Kari a lemonade, then sat down on the chinz-covered settee adjacent to Kari.

"Why are you asking me? How should I know?" The girl snapped, instantly repenting. "I'm sorry Grandma. I didn't mean—"

"No, it's none of my business. Old women have the tendency to butt in where they're not—"

Kari slipped from the rocker to Grandma's feet. "Please, I am sorry. But there's nothing between Marc and me. We're friends, that's all."

"Well, if there's not, there should be. What's wrong with that boy? Lost his senses or his eyesight? I can see that you haven't. Oops! I'm butting in again, aren't I?" Grandma smirked devilishly.

Kari arched a disapproving eyebrow, grinned, and shook her head. "You said it, I didn't." Kari had decided long ago that nothing would cure Grandma of her endless matchmaking schemes.

"When you get to be my age and have high blood pressure, high cholesterol, high blood sugar, heart trouble, arthritis, and whatever else one can name, butting in is the only pleasure left."

"OK, Grandma, I'll level with you. You're right. I do care for Marc, much more than I should. It's just that over the years, my opinion of men hasn't been too healthy. My mother's taste in the masculine gender is infamous for being faulty." Kari paused, studying the lemon pulp lining the sides of her glass. "It's a long, sordid story—not very pretty. Many times if it hadn't been for Mom Wynter's sister, Amanda, I don't know what I would have done. She thought that getting away from the city for a summer might help me heal, and that I could be a big help to Mom Wynters."

"And you have been, my dear," Grandma insisted.

"I'd intended to find my own place and apply for a job at the local hospital. Instead, I opted for country living." Kari paused, allowing time for a new thought to form in her mind. "You know, getting to know Dad Wynters has challenged all my previous notions concerning men. And I do see many of those same fine qualities in Marc. Regardless, right now I still need space and time to examine my own thinking without the pressure of a romantic entanglement," she added. "So does Marc, I think."

Grandma nodded. "You're probably wise. I just know that I've been married to three good men. All preceded me in death, and if I weren't a knockin' on death's door myself right now, I'd marry again."

Kari couldn't believe the old woman.

Grandma chuckled at the girl's shocked expression. "I'll admit there's a lot of misery in the world caused by bad marriages, but that doesn't mean one should throw the baby out with the bath water! Look at the happiness available to couples that love the Lord and love one another too."

"Grandma, you're a crafty lady, do you know that?" Kari clucked. "Anyway, fortunately or unfortunately, whichever happens to be the case from your perspective, Marc and I are just friends. But as for you, I understand that Mr. Moses down by the Gadsby place is just about the right age. I could drop a gentle hint now and then when I see him in town."

Grandma started indignantly. "That old coot? Why he's got one foot in the grave and the other on a banana peel."

Kari hugged the sputtering woman tightly. "OK, let's make a deal. You run your love life and I'll run mine. How's that?"

"You've got a deal!" Something in the twinkle in Grandma's eyes warned Kari not to completely trust the old woman's sudden acquiescence.

"I've got to be heading back to the farm, Grandma." Kari said. "The Wynters are attending a Grange potluck tonight, and Mom might need my help. I'll be back next week to check up on you. And remember your promise, young lady—no matchmaking!" Kari slipped the basket handle over her arm and headed for the door.

"You run along now. Give my love to Mindy and to her Mama." Grandma followed Kari outside and waved from the porch.

The trees arching the driveway relieved the high temperatures of the direct sunlight. It would be hours before the thermometer dropped as much as ten degrees. "I need a cold shower," she mused as she parked the truck in front of the large white farmhouse. "A dip in the river would be even nicer. It sure feels good to be home." Kari bounded up the front steps and through the screen door.

"Hi, anybody home?"

Only the gentle tick of the hall clock broke the silence.

"Hmm, I guess they all decided to go to the potluck." She ran up the stairs to her room. On her bed lay two letters. Kari stopped in surprise. One was from Amanda, the other from Sheena. How far away they both seemed, Amanda by distance and her mother in every way possible.

She read Amanda's letter first. She enjoyed reading of all the latest happenings in the small inner city church they'd attended together. Amanda described how six-year-old Megan lost her two front teeth and how four-year-old Sammy had discovered artichokes. "He eats them like a gourmet."

Reluctantly Kari opened her mother's letter, the first she'd received since she left home over two months before. Kari dreaded the thought. All her memories were so terrible. She hated dredging them up again through Sheena's letter.

"Dear Kari,
This is just a short note begging you to come home. I need your help. I fell down the stairs and broke my leg in three places."

"More likely Keith broke it while beating you up!" Kari muttered.

"Since I get out of the hospital in a few days and I'm still in a cast, I'll need someone to care for me. You, being a nurse and all, would be a big help around here.

"By the way, Keith left me the day after the accident and hasn't been back since. I don't know where he is. And right now, I don't care.

"Please, you can have your old room back. I won't mention one word about your new-found religion, or Keith, or try to interfere in your life in any way. You can go to church whenever you like. And you can go to visit your friend Amanda also without any complaints from me, I promise.

"What do you say? I really need you, baby. Doesn't your religion say something about 'honoring fathers and mothers'? Well, here's your chance to live it.

Love,
Sheena"

Angry beyond words, Kari crumpled the letter and threw it across the room in the general direction of the wastebasket. "How dare she!" Kari screamed. "Of all the audacious, rotten angles to take—my religion! After the torment she put me through? And Keith, that worm! I can have my room back—who wants it?"

"I can't go. I won't go! No, Lord, please don't ask me to!" Kari wailed, throwing herself across the bed and pounding the bed pillow. Within minutes, she had sobbed herself to sleep.

Hours later a mosquito buzzing round her head awakened her. Slap! She missed. She waved the pest away again only to have it return. How she had laughed last month when the natives joked about mounting machine guns on their silos to counter attack the hungry little monsters. But after a number of encounters of her own, she learned to respect the mosquitoes' territory, which meant anywhere the pesky insects might choose to fly.

As the sun's last rays streaked through her window, she watched a flock of birds congregate in the oak tree on the other side of the drive-way and listened to their discordant concert. As if on cue, the birds flew to their nests, leaving an eerie silence behind.

Kari was surprised when she heard orchestral music drift up the stair-well. She decided that the folks must have gotten back from their Grange meeting. Yawning, she made her way down to the parlor. "Hi, when did you folks re— ? Oh, it's you. I didn't hear you come in."

"I live here, remember?" Marc teased. "Want some maple nut ice cream?" He held out a large cereal bowlfull.

Kari demured. "No thanks, you go ahead. I just came down to get a glass of orange juice. I've got some letters to answer."

"Forget the letters. I'm bored. Let's go for a walk." Marc tipped his head to one side.

"The mosquitoes—" Kari began.

"There's a breeze by now. They won't bother us. Come on," he teased, stuffing another spoonful of ice cream into his mouth.

"But if your folks come back they'll be worried," Kari stammered.

Marc arched his eyebrows in surprise. "I doubt it. We *are* friends, re-member? Are you afraid to be alone with me or something?"

Kari laughed at the obvious challenge in his voice. "Of course not. Don't be ridiculous."

She turned and ran up the stairs to her room. Her mother's discarded letter lay crumpled on the floor beside the waste basket. Ignoring it, Kari changed clothes, berating herself as she bustled about the room. "You idiot, don't go!"

Quickly, she slipped into a pink calico sundress and ran a brush through her curls, catching them at the nape of her neck with a match-ing ribbon. She checked her image in the mirror. "Must everything be serious? Can't you just relax and enjoy Marc's companionship? Stop turning everything into a major crisis!" Kari tucked a stray curl under the ribbon and ran down the stairs to Marc.

# Chapter 8
# A Time to Decide

Kari and Marc ambled along the dark road that edged the harvested field. "I just love Wisconsin's clear night skies," she said.

"Yeah, I miss it sometimes when I'm back at school," Marc admitted. "In Michigan, the skies are more often cloudy."

Kari stumbled over a dirt clod. Marc reached out to catch her arm. "Careful. Wisconsin stardust can do that to you, you know."

Kari laughed. "It sure can," she thought, deciding it best to change the subject. "I wish I knew the names of all the constellations. Do you know many of them?"

"A few," he replied. "I took an astronomy course last quarter just for the fun of it." They came to a small rise in the road and stopped.

"All I can identify are the Big and Little Dippers, and the North Star, of course," Kari said ruefully.

One by one, Marc pointed out the most visible constellations. As the blinking lights from a jet passed over, Marc placed his hand on Kari's shoulder and pointed to the north. "One night, when I was about nine years old, Dad and I came out here to watch the northern lights. They danced like a laser light show. I'll never forget it. I like to come here when I want to be alone."

Kari stiffened. "Oh, I'm sorry. Perhaps—"

"No, if I didn't want you along, I wouldn't have invited you."

"Look! Over there!" Kari's head swung about suddenly. "A shooting star. I don't think I've ever seen one before."

Instead of following the star's progress, Marc took her hand. She tried to pull away. "No, don't run away from me again, please."

"But—"

"I realize that our friendship had a rough beginning, but I do want you to know how much I've enjoyed the good times we've had together this summer." He released her hand and folded his arms across his chest.

"Too many romances are destroyed by long distances. It happened to my roommate last year, and I determined it wouldn't happen to me."

Kari froze. "What is he trying to say?" she wondered. She pursed her lips in an attempt to choose her words carefully. "You're a special kind of guy, Marc. Some lucky gal will snap you up in a minute when you hit campus this fall."

Marc grunted and continued. "You've become rather special to me too." A comfortable silence settled between them as they watched the constantly changing night sky.

Kari's thoughts tumbled over one another as she thought of her mother's request, of leaving the Wynters, of saying goodbye to Marc especially. Finally, she spoke. "I imagine you'll be glad to get back to school."

"Oh yeah, it will be great to finish at last," Marc admitted.

"Just think, in little more than a week the night sky will change for both of us. You'll be studying the stars in Michigan's sky and I'll be back in Chicago, where smog blocks out even the brightest of stars."

Marc grabbed Kari's arm. "What did you say?"

Kari began again. "I said that in a little more than a week—"

"I heard what you said. I just don't understand. I thought Mom asked you to stay here for the winter, to apply for a job at the Beaver Dam Hospital."

"She did, but I received a letter today. I've been thinking about it all evening. My mother needs me. I've decided to leave for Chicago by the end of the week." Kari's eyes glistened with tears. The sudden silence between them was deafening. "I'll miss you all of course, but, well, I have obligations."

Kari could hear Marc heave a series of deep, tense breaths, as if searching for something to say.

"Look, I'll be all right there. Keith is gone."

Marc snapped his head toward Kari. "Keith? Who's Keith?"

"Oops." Kari cleared her throat and swallowed. "Um, I guess you'd call him my stepfather."

Kari could feel Marc's eyes boring into the side of her head. "Is he the reason you came to Wisconsin in the first place?"

"Uh, yes." Kari hesitated. "You could say that. He, and the fact that my mother kicked me out."

Marc grabbed her by the shoulders and whirled her around to face him. "And you're going back? I don't believe it!" Marc searched her face for answers.

Her eyes pleaded with him to understand. "What choice do I have? I'm the only practicing Christian my mother ever knew. I have to go back. I owe her that much."

Marc released her shoulders before he spoke, his voice husky with emotion. "I think you're making a terrible mistake." He jammed his fists into his hip pockets and turned. His profile silhouetted in the starlight. Kari could make out the hardened lines of his jaw.

She shrugged and whispered, "But it *is* my decision to make."

"Hmmph!"

Kari bristled. "Marc, are you aware that you are a bully with women?" Marc spun around and faced her. "I'm a what?"

"A bully!" Kari's jaw jutted out defiantly. "That's right. Every chance you get, you start trying to tell me what to do, how to think, everything! I am incensed by it."

Marc's face suffused with anger. "Why—" he sputtered.

"Maybe you expect to find a cute little coed that will subject herself to your thinking in order to be seen with you, but not me, brother!" Kari had the urge to stamp her foot in emphasis. "I appreciate your advice. I appreciate your concern. But I do not appreciate your bullying."

"Well, I certainly will not presume on *our* friendship any longer!"

"Good!" Kari nodded emphatically. "Because that's the only basis we have for maintaining this friendship. And I would appreciate it if you would allow me to be the one to tell your folks, OK?"

"Sure!" Marc snapped. "You're one stubborn woman, Kari Gerard."

Kari waited for Marc to say more. He didn't. "Why, Marc? Because I don't kowtow to your directives? I'm not that kind of person. I can't afford to be. Except for God, I'm alone in the world. I've got to be stubborn to survive. I can't let others make my decisions, as pleasant as it sometimes sounds."

"Hmmph!" Marc snorted.

Kari smiled in spite of herself at Marc's stock reply whenever he couldn't refute her arguments. "Can't you understand?" She turned toward the house. "I'm going back. It's been a long day."

"Sure!" Marc sighed, then turned away.

Kari stumbled down the road. "How can I expect him to understand? I don't even understand," she thought. "I can't allow myself to become like Sheena, so totally dependent on a man that I'd renounce my own daughter rather than risk losing him. No! I won't be that kind of woman. Nor do I want to love a man like Keith who would demand such base loyalty. But then, is Marc really like that? I don't know. I just don't know." She fought to hold back her tears, but lost the battle when she reached the porch steps and Mindy.

"Hi, where've you been? We got home over an hour ago and couldn't find you or Marc anywhere." Sudden understanding dawned on Mindy, and she gulped. "Oops! Sorry!"

"Don't be. We just took a walk, and I decided I'd had enough and came back alone. I'm sure he will be along any minute." Fearing she might lose her nerve if she waited, Kari continued, "Where are your mom and dad? I need to talk with them."

"They're in the family room watching TV." Mindy eyed Kari suspiciously. "What's wrong?"

"Wrong? What can be wrong?" Kari recountered, immediately regretting the sharp tone in her voice.

Mindy's blue eyes widened at the attack. "I'm sorry. You just look upset, that's all."

"Hey, I'm sorry too," Kari apologized. "Thanks for caring, but everything is great, *just great.*" Kari smiled weakly and walked inside the house. She rubbed her palms nervously along the sides of her skirt and tried to swallow the lump hardening in her throat. She paused at the doorway. "Mom? Dad? May I speak with both of you for a moment?"

"Sure honey. Did you have a good evening?" Mom glanced up as Kari entered the room. A frown immediately knitted her brow. "What's the matter, Kari? You've been crying."

"I . . . I . . . I received a letter from my mother today. It seems that she broke her leg. She has asked me to come home to care for her, and, well, I think that I should go." Kari's voice caught in her throat.

Mom gasped. "Oh, I'm so sorry. Of course you should go to her. She's your mother, and she needs you."

Dad reached over and turned off the television. "Now what's this all about?"

He listened as Kari related the contents of her mother's letter. "We'll miss you terribly. You *will* come back to us when she gets better, won't you?"

Kari sniffed and turned away. "I—I'm not sure of my plans as yet. I may get my own apartment and apply for a nursing job at one of the local hospitals. I just don't know right now; I'm terribly confused." Kari struggled to control a new flood of tears brimming in her eyes.

Mom sprang to Kari's side and engulfed the girl in her arms. "Of course you are. How terrible for you."

"Have you prayed about this?" Dad questioned. "Are you sure the Lord wants you to go back into that environment?"

"Now, Marcus, we don't have any idea what the Lord's plans are for Kari. But we do know that He'll be with her, even in Chicago."

Kari ran her hand across her aching forehead. "You've both been so good to me, but it's time I got on with my life. I'm almost twenty years old. I can't sponge off other people any longer." Kari straightened.

"Sponge? You've worked as hard as any of us," Mom scolded. "Family, that's what we are, family, and you're a vital part of it. Sponge, indeed!"

The front door slammed. Marc stormed into the house and up the stairs.

"Marc? Marc, is everything all right?" Dad Wynters called, then turned toward Kari. "What's going on here? First you come in all teary eyed, announcing your sudden departure. Then my son bursts into the house like an angry bull and heads straight for his room. Is he the reason you're leaving?" Dad Wynters eyed first Kari, then his wife. "I'm getting to the bottom of this."

"Don't! Please! What I told you is true. The letter is up in my room if you want to read it. I think I'm doing what is best." Her voice trembled with emotion. "Please, try to understand," Kari pleaded. "It's taking every bit of strength I have to leave. You've been so good to me. I love both of you so much."

For once, Dad Wynters backed down. "All right. If that's truly the way you want it."

Kari nodded her head slowly. "This is the way I want it."

During her last weekend in the Wynters' home, Kari changed her mind almost hourly about returning to Chicago, but always returned to the conviction that she was doing the right thing by leaving. While Marc avoided Kari, Mindy tagged after her wherever she went until Mom had to order her daughter to stop.

Michael voiced his disapproval of her leaving on the way home from grocery shopping on Wednesday. "Shucks," he half joked, "I'd hoped, with Marc gone this fall I'd have a chance with you."

"Thanks, Michael, for the compliment, but I keep telling you that there's nothing beyond friendship between Marc and me." Kari patted his arm. "And you'll always be a pretty special friend to me, too, even after you've found yourself that pretty blue-eyed blonde."

"What blonde?"

"The one you're going to meet at school this fall," Kari teased. "Seriously, I'll come back to visit occasionally."

"But it won't be the same, will it?"

"Nothing ever remains the same, Michael." Kari planted a tender kiss on his blushing cheek.

Kari dreaded her last visit with Grandma Lewis. She realized how much the frail old woman appreciated her weekly visits—not only the companionship the younger woman gave but Kari's medical knowledge as well.

Grandma Lewis ushered Kari indoors in her usual ebullient style.

"I want you to know that I have faith in your good judgment," she said. "And though I dread having you leave, my prayers will go with you." She motioned Kari to her favorite rocker. "And as far as Marc is concerned, I hope I didn't offend you. It's just that Marc and I have always been buddies. I kind of look out for his best interest."

"Oh?" Kari walked slowly to the chair and sat down.

"I've been wrong to push you two together," Grandma continued. "God needs to be the one who brings two young people together, not a selfish old woman."

Kari leaned forward in the rocker. "You're not a selfish old woman— far from it."

Grandma Lewis nodded thoughtfully.

Kari studied her hands. "I dread returning to my mother's apartment more than you'll ever know. But she really does need me. She's all alone. I can't turn my back on her."

"Of course you can't. I know that now. But I admit that I will miss the sunshine you bring into my life each week."

Kari rose from the chair and crossed to Grandma's side. "I love you so much. You've helped me in so many ways."

"One thing I want you to know before you go. If things become difficult between you and your mother, I would love to have you live here with me." Grandma's eyes misted as she lifted her rough, gnarled hand to Kari's moist cheek. "In the meantime, do what you must do, and go with God."

"Go with God. Go with God," Kari thought. "Yes, right choice or wrong, I've learned to confidently go with God."

On Friday morning Mom insisted that the entire family come to the train depot to see Kari off. Kari would much rather have said goodbye to everyone at the house with less fanfare, but that was not to be. Fortunately, whether by her doing or his, Kari had no time alone with Marc.

Her cheerful mask stayed securely in place throughout the long drive to the station. Marc and Michael each grabbed her luggage and checked it in at the station for her. Mindy, unusually silent, hung close to Kari's arm while Mom chatted on, giving advice and talking about the trip she'd made by train to Omaha for a Grange convention.

When Michael and Marc returned from the platform, Dad called the family together. "Let's walk out onto the platform and form a prayer circle."

Mindy's eyes widened in surprise. "Here?"

"Sure, why not?" he grinned, leading the way. Mindy shrugged and tagged along.

They all joined hands at one end of the platform. Kari contrasted the warm softness of Mindy's hand to her left with Michael's rougher, calloused hand on her right. She managed to avoid Marc's gaze directly across from her as he stood between his parents.

"Dear Father, We thank you this day for families, for each member of our family standing in this circle. Our circle will be getting smaller, first with Kari's departure, then with Marc's. We feel especially blessed for the privilege of adding Kari to our family this summer. She's been a joy to us. It was family that brought her to us, and now, a member of her family is taking her away for a time." He cleared his throat and went on. "And so I ask that a special blessing go with her. Guide her. Help her to always remember that wherever she may go, she's never alone, that Your promises are true, and that she will always hold a special place in our hearts. And if it is Your will, Father, bring her back to us someday. Amen."

The whistle of the incoming train hastened their goodbyes. Kari kissed Mom gently. "Thank you for everything. You have been more like a mother to me than you can possibly know. I've learned so much about just everything." Kari hugged her tightly.

Mom took Kari's face between her hands. "When you have everything settled, write. Keep in touch."

"I agree. Let us know how you are doing. It won't be the same with you gone." Dad slid his arm around Kari's shoulders and squeezed.

The conductor from the train bellowed. "All aboard! Express leaving for Milwaukee and all points East."

Mindy threw her arms around Kari. "I'm gonna miss you so much."

"Come on Michael and Marc," Dad laughed. "You might as well get in on this sob session too."

After receiving a peck on her cheek from Michael, Kari turned to pick up her travel case. Instead, a long, bronzed arm extended past hers, lifted the case, and handed it to her.

"Bye, kid." Marc's deep blue eyes searched Kari's thoughtfully.

Kari swallowed hard, took a deep breath, then pasted a broad smile on her face. "Hey, thanks for everything. I always wanted a big brother. You've been great." Kari hoped that her voice wouldn't give her away.

"Big brother?" He drawled, kissing her gently on the tip of her nose. "That's a new twist. I hadn't quite thought of our relationship in that light." Marc tapped her jaw playfully with his fist. "Friends?"

"Friends," she answered.

He tipped his head to one side and squinted, facing the midmorning sun. "Maybe I'll stop by to see you on my way to the university. You wouldn't mind, would you?"

"Mind?" Kari swallowed hard. "Why should I mind? Sounds great. And I'm sure that your Aunt Amanda would be thrilled to see you."

The train signaled its imminent departure. "Saved by the bell," Kari thought as she whirled about, throwing kisses and waving goodbye to the only real family she'd ever known.

"I won't cry! I won't cry! I won't cry!" Kari determined as the train eased out of the station while the building cadence of the wheels on the rails clacked, "Yes, you will, Yes, you will, Yes, you will!"

# Chapter 9
# Chicago Again

Kari hurried past the decaying brownstone houses lining the sidewalk of southwest Chicago. At the sight of a gang of teenage boys gathered on the street corner she stepped up her pace. A thick layer of clouds cast a gray hue over the entire neighborhood. Even the cars, illegally parked along the side of the street, seemed to be painted the same muddy grays and browns as the rest of the neighborhood. She stopped in front of the row house that had been her home for so many years. "Well, here goes." She paused, took a deep breath, as if inhaling an added dose of courage, then started up the three flights of stairs to her mother's apartment.

"Hello there, Kari," round-faced Mrs. Dumont called from her open doorway. "We've missed you. Your mother said that you'd gone to the country. Are you home for good now?"

"Probably so. It's good to see you too. How are those twins of yours doing, Joey and Jeremy, isn't it?" Kari climbed the flight of stairs as she talked.

The woman smiled, pleased that Kari remembered. "That's right. Growing like weeds. Come on down later. I know they'd be tickled to see you again."

Kari turned and smiled. "I just might, once I know how much help my mother needs, what with her broken leg and all," she answered. Kari almost missed the look of disgust on Mrs. Dumont's face at the mention of her mother. "I guess it's been difficult now that Keith's gone."

A short silence followed as Mrs. Dumont scratched at an invisible speck of dirt on the doorjamb. "We'll be home all evening, but come down and see us anytime."

Upon reaching the third floor, Kari sighed with despair. After three months in the wide open spaces of Wisconsin the dark, graffiti-scarred walls closed in, threatening to smother her. She stopped at the door, raised her fist to knock, then hesitated. She knew that once she knocked on the door, she would have passed the point of no return. "No," she reasoned, "I did that 175 miles ago at the Columbus, Wisconsin, depot."

"Sheena, it's me—Kari. I'm home," she called, knocking on the apartment door. She listened as footsteps approached, and the door swung open. On the couch at the far side of the room sat her mother, immobilized by a heavy cast as Kari had expected. But the unshaven, unkept individual leaning insolently against the doorjamb came as a nightmarish rerun of every horror she'd ever imagined.

"Keith!" Kari started. "Mother, you told me that he left you."

"So I came back to my everloving old lady," Keith sneered. "This is *my* place, you know."

Kari remained glued to the threshold, suitcase in hand. "Look, Mother, I agreed to help you only because you wrote that you had no one. Now that Keith's here, I'll return to Wisconsin."

"Is that any way to greet your invalid mother?" Sheena pouted. Her disheveled, bleached-blond hair streaked down across her full red mouth, partially hiding the dark rings circling her dull, listless eyes. As usual, a number of discarded wine bottles lay abandoned on the floor around the sofa.

"At least come and give me a kiss. Doesn't your God say something about loving your parents?" Her mother extended her arms. Kari bristled at the flippant reference to her faith, but obeyed.

"Keith, get Kari and me a root beer," Sheena ordered. Keith fired angry darts at Kari and stomped from the room.

"Look, I'm sorry, baby, but Keith just showed up here today. Honest, I wouldn't have brought you home if I'd known he would return. You must know that!" Sheena's dark eyes flashed with the same anger she'd hurled at Kari three months earlier. "And I do need you and your medical skills."

Kari glanced around the slovenly kept room. Except for the cast on her mother's leg, nothing had changed. Except for the cast, and Kari. "How did I miss seeing things as they really were for so long?" Kari shuddered to herself. "I can't live in a pigsty like this!"

"You need a live-in maid, Mother, not a nurse." Kari removed a stack of dirty clothes from the soiled green recliner chair and placed them on the coffee table atop numerous layers of old magazines, dirty plates, and empty potato chip bags. Then she sat down. "Tell me about your injury."

Sheena looked nervously toward Keith and began. "Well, it was on a Saturday night. Keith and I had just come home from Andy's Bar and Grill down on Fourth Street. We'd been arguing, and I admit that I was a little tipsy." She gestured with her hand. "We'd almost reached the second landing, and Keith says I staggered. I don't remember too good. He tried to grab me, but I fell the entire flight of stairs. I woke up in Westside General Hospital two days later with a concussion and a leg broken in three places."

One look at Keith told Kari all she needed to know. His guilt was obvious, as was his lack of repentance. Kari harbored no doubt that he'd pushed Sheena, or at the least could have prevented her fall. She also recognized the same disgusting leer in the man's eyes.

She closed her eyes, trying to concentrate on the rest of her mother's story, but her mind floundered, searching for an escape. "What should I do?" she thought. "Go back to Wisconsin? Hardly. I can't sponge off the Wynters any longer, no matter what they say. Move in with Amanda and the kids? No, no room, and I'd still be depending on others. Get a job and my own apartment? But how soon can I afford to do that? One month? Two?" Whatever the answer, Kari knew she could not stay here now that Keith was back. "Just the thought of him makes my skin crawl," she muttered, unable to hide her disgust.

"Remember," Kari could almost hear Mom Wynters speaking, "God loves Keith as much as He does you."

"What a terrible thought!" Kari blushed, knowing she almost spoke the thought aloud. Her mother continued relating the details of her injury as Kari daydreamed about the afternoon in the middle of the onion patch when she'd spilled the entire story to Mom Wynters.

"I can forgive my mother's alcoholism," she explained. "I've lived with that all my life. It's the physical and verbal abuse Keith hurls when he's drunk, and his sickening passes that Mama accuses me of instigating, that I can't stand."

The memory of that summer afternoon was so vivid that even in her mother's living room Kari could almost hear the honeybees buzzing around her head. She snapped back to the present. Her gaze drifted over the torn fiberglass draperies ill hung on the bay window, the water stains on the wallpaper, and Keith, the object of her disgust. Wordlessly, she prayed. "Father, if You love him so much, then somehow I guess I'll have to also. Is that why I was brought back here, to this environment? Was Wisconsin only a short reprieve? Will I ever be able to go back?" The thought that Marc might be out of her life forever depressed her more than she'd ever imagined possible. She sank deeper into the chair, opening the can of root beer Keith carelessly tossed her way.

"Kari, are you listening? I said that you can have your own room back, baby," Sheena consoled, her hands fidgeting with the moth-eaten afghan slung across her lap. "Everything's just the way you left it."

Kari leaned forward in the chair. "Not everything, Mother." She took a deep breath. "I want you to know that I will stay here only until you can get up and around on your own. And I think it would be best if I go job hunting tomorrow morning. That will enable me to eventually rent a place of my own. You and Keith don't need a grown daughter hanging around to complicate your lives."

"But, baby, I need you here, with me," Sheena whined, brushing her tangled hair from her face.

"Don't worry, Keith and I will work out a schedule where one of us will be with you all the time, won't we, Keith?" Kari glared at Keith, daring him to defy her suggestion. He continued to sulk.

"Well, another paycheck would help a lot." Sheena's eyes narrowed greedily.

"No, Mother! No cash. I won't buy you any booze. I figure that my nursing skills will more than make up for the cost of housing me. And I will, of course, contribute to the groceries. I have an entirely new supply of wholesome recipes that Mom Wynters gave me. You'll love them. And you look like you could use a balanced meal." The memory of Mom Wynters' gentle face brought tears to Kari's eyes.

Sheena clutched her soiled robe about her chest defensively. "I've managed."

"Yes, you have, but now with Keith and me taking turns helping you, you can concentrate on getting well and leave the worrying to us." Kari ignored Keith standing shadowed in the bay window, sullenly watching and listening. "Everything's going to be just fine, so don't you worry."

The gelatinlike quivering in Kari's stomach belied her confidence. She felt trapped, alone. She knew that she wouldn't abandon her mother. She also knew that any help supplied by Keith would be strictly a bonus, since he seldom remained sober enough to work, hence collect a paycheck. Why he hadn't been fired long ago from his job at the factory she couldn't figure out.

Kari walked across to the television and switched it on. "I'm going to go to my room and get settled. I'm pretty tired. I'll probably turn in early tonight. Oh, by the way, Keith, is the screwdriver still in the kitchen cabinet beside the sink? I bought a convenient little lock that I want to install before I sleep tonight." She arched one eyebrow, certain he'd caught the inference.

After the last of her clothing had been placed in the bureau, Kari slipped beneath the clean sheets she'd put on her bed, took her Bible from the nightstand, and began to read from Psalm 92.

" 'It is a good thing to give thanks unto the Lord, and to sing praises unto Thy name, O most High.' "

"I'm sorry, Lord, I've been whining about my lot in life, forgetting all the blessings You gave me through my stay at the Wynters. If You are asking me to pass that love on now to my mother . . . and to Keith, I will do so cheerfully, without complaining!"

Later that night Kari lay in her bed, trying to tune out the now unfamiliar noises of the restless city. In their place she tried to hear the soothing sounds of the farm. But like vapor in the wind, they eluded her. Instead, Marc's silhouette against a star-studded sky etched itself into her consciousness. She finally fell asleep and slept fitfully most of the night between dreams about Marc.

Accustomed to rising with the sun and to making big breakfasts, Kari awakened at 6:30 and began to plot out her plan of attack. An hour later the apartment was filled with the aroma of homemade pancakes and scrambled eggs. When her mother and Keith finally emerged from their bedroom, she noted their shock at discovering a neat and orderly parlor and kitchen. Even the dining room table gleamed from a fresh polishing. A vase containing plastic daisies occupied the center of the table. With the help of an old flowered skirt she'd found in her closet and a pair of pinking shears, Kari designed four attractive placemats and was busy setting the table with the mismatched tableware and plates she'd located in the kitchen cupboards.

"What's going on here?" Sheena stood in the archway between the parlor and dining room, leaning on Keith's arm, and rubbing her obviously throbbing head. She looked confused and irritated.

"Breakfast! I hope I didn't make too much. I'm used to feeding an army, I'm afraid," Kari apologized. "Now, Mama, you sit down here at the end of the table. That way you can extend your cast to one side a lot easier. Keith and I will sit across from one another. There, that's it." Kari could tell that neither Keith nor Sheena knew quite how to handle the situation. She watched Sheena struggle to remain irate. Regardless of the woman's hangover, her curiosity was piqued.

"Where did you get those flowers?" Sheena demanded.

"I, uh, stripped them from that plastic bouquet you had sitting on the TV set and rearranged them. You don't mind, do you? After we eat I'll put them back if you like. As soon as I get a job we'll have live ones," Kari promised. "At the Wynters, I fell in love with daisies. They grew everywhere all summer long. Those stubborn little plants flourished even where the ground was rock solid and overworked. I learned to admire their tenacity."

"Are you going to talk all day long, or are we gonna eat?" Keith snarled, a fork in one hand, a knife in the other.

"After we say grace." She bowed her head before either could object. Finishing her prayer, she scurried to the kitchen and carried the food to the table. During the meal she refused to let them bait her. When tempted to fire back a nasty retort she glanced at the daisies, smiled to herself, and continued eating.

She studied Keith as he wolfed down his food. She couldn't help comparing his bestial behavior with Dad Wynters' and Marc's manly countenances. She decided that if the humanists had only Keith to study, it was easy to see why they believed people evolved from apes. Kari checked her unexpected giggle with a bite of buttered pancake.

"Well," Sheena pushed back from the table and sighed contentedly, "You've become quite a cook. Everything tasted terrific."

Kari blushed at the unfamiliar compliment coming from her mother. "Thanks. Thanks a lot. Oh yes, I almost forgot. Keith, I'll have the potatoes cleaned and in the oven before I leave for job hunting. And I'll set the oven temperature. If you could be sure to start the oven at four this afternoon, I'd appreciate it." Keith grunted and left the table. Sheena followed, complaining of a severe headache.

Kari whistled as she cleaned the stove and put away the last of the breakfast dishes, all the while mentally listing the jobs she wanted to accomplish in the days to come. "Hmm, yes, those kitchen curtains definitely need washing, possibly replacing. And the window! Mom Wynters would have fits if she saw those layers of grease coating the panes. But for now, I'd better get dressed and hit the hospital personnel offices."

# Chapter 10
# The Empty Cash Box

Kari dropped her jacket on the the bed in her room after an exhausting night on the eleven-to-seven shift at Harris Memorial Hospital. She had been relieved to learn that her schedule and Keith's barely overlapped. And though more often irritable than not, even Sheena grudgingly admitted to liking some of Kari's healthful meals.

It was the letters from Wisconsin, news from home telling about Mindy's new braces, Dad's new pickup truck, or about a new colt born during the first snowstorm of the season, along with her weekly visits to Amanda, that sustained Kari and kept her sane. After attending church services each week she gratefully accepted Amanda's invitation to spend the day with her and the children, away from Sheena and Keith. Usually Kari stayed until time to report for work at the hospital.

One evening as Kari waited for Amanda to finish putting the children to bed she browsed through the family album that Amanda kept on the coffee table. Her eyes grew misty when she came to a picture of Marc as a toddler, sitting in the middle of an inflatable kiddy pool, trying to drink from a hose. She bit her lip as a familiar ache coursed through her.

"It was Marc, wasn't it?"

Kari turned, surprised to see Amanda standing behind the couch. "What are you talking about?" Kari flipped to the next page in the album.

Amanda walked around the end of the couch and sat down beside her. "You know what I mean. Marc was part of the reason you left Wisconsin."

"I came home to help my mother," Kari defended.

"Partly perhaps, but you become so silent whenever his name is mentioned. Besides, my sister Ruth sort of hinted at it in her last letter."

"That's ridiculous. I never discussed my feelings for Marc with—" Kari stopped midsentence and reddened.

"Please, Amanda, I'd rather not—" For Kari, the floodgates had been opened, and though she tried, she couldn't stop herself. She knew she needed to talk with someone, someone who really cared and could understand. Amanda qualified on both counts, Amanda who had loved and lost—Amanda who understood disillusionment and sorrow.

"I did come home because of Sheena. But you're right, Marc unwittingly influenced my final decision. As you've already guessed, there was a spark between us from the moment he met me at the depot last spring. But it was a— Oh, I don't know— a sparring contest almost. Early on we both agreed that neither wanted anything more than a friendship." Kari folded her knees up beneath her chin. "Marc didn't want a long-distance relationship, and well, you know why I was against any involvement!"

Amanda tipped her head to one side. "No. Why?"

"Tsk, come on," Kari began. "After all my mother's paramours, Keith being the latest?"

"What does that have to do with you or with Marc?"

"Everything! I won't allow myself to be used and abused like my mother." Kari swiped at a strand of hair that had fallen across her cheek. "Men! They're all alike. You know that."

Amanda grunted. "I know no such thing. I was married to a good Christian man. My sister is married to one also. Don't you agree?"

Kari swallowed hard. "Well, yes, of course. Dad Wynters is a gem."

"And Marc is his son!"

Kari buried her head in her arms. Of course Amanda would say that. Wasn't Marc her nephew? Yet inwardly Kari knew Amanda spoke the truth. Marc and Keith were different, very different. So many times since she left Wisconsin Kari had told herself that very thing. She wanted to trust Marc, but how could she? There had been no commitment on his part, nor on hers. Perhaps what he felt for her was purely physical, like Keith, just not as obnoxious. "How will I know? How can I ever be certain?" She wondered.

Kari leaned back against the couch and continued sharing her thoughts with Amanda. Her friend listened, asking pertinent questions along the way. When she finished, Kari waited expectantly.

"In all thy ways acknowledge him, and he shall direct thy paths," Amanda recited. "Sounds simplistic, doesn't it?"

Kari nodded her head in agreement.

Amanda pursed her lips thoughtfully, then reached for Kari's hands. "That's a promise I depend on daily since my husband died. And whether God intends for you and Marc to get together, I don't know. Yet God's promise will still hold true, if you claim it."

"Oh, by the way," Amanda continued, "My sister wants us to spend Thanksgiving with them in Wisconsin. She said you'd be getting a letter in a day or so. Marc can pick us up on his way home from the university."

Kari frowned and bit her lower lip. "Amanda, Mindy wrote and told me that Marc is dating a girl named Yvonne. She thinks they might even be engaged by Christmas." Kari picked at an imaginary catch in one of her fingernails. Her eyes watered at the sympathizing pain she read in her friend's eyes.

"I'm sorry," Amanda began.

Kari brushed a tear aside and hastened to change the subject. "Sheena will have her cast off next week. Then I'll feel free to leave. I've saved enough money to rent an efficiency apartment near the hospital. Maybe I'll wait to move until we return from Wisconsin." Pasting a smile in place, Kari sighed, "It's about time I get on with my life, don't you think?"

"If that's what you want." The older woman shook her head sadly.

"What I want doesn't seem to be— I'm sorry. I said I wouldn't complain anymore, and I won't start now. Did I tell you that Sheena has been asking me to read to her from my Bible? Isn't that remarkable? Even Keith sneaked into the parlor yesterday and listened."

Kari thought for a moment then jumped up from the couch, placing her hands on her hips. "Where did you say that recipe was for lemon gelatin cake?"

"Has the lock worked?" Amanda questioned as she led the way to the tiny kitchenette.

"Absolutely. The lock was such a simple idea, and it has worked ever so well." Kari turned and smiled at Amanda. "Thanks for the idea. I don't know why I didn't think of it. Most of the time I'm at work during the night, so it's no problem. The one night Keith forced his way into my room I panicked, I guess. Of course he never bothers me unless he's drunk. Then he's either amorous or belligerent. Neither are very desirable moods. I think he's more than a little intimidated by my bossiness too. I confess that I've completely taken over the running of the household. Even Sheena defers to my judgment on almost everything— everything, that is, except her booze."

"Well, I'll be glad when you're finally out of there. I think you're doing the right thing getting your own place. It will be rough at times meeting all the bills, but you can do it," Amanda assured her. "And I'll help whenever I can."

"I wish the job held more promise though. I'm only a fill-in for a nurse that took a one-year sabbatical to finish her midwifery course. When she returns in January I might be out of work entirely. I don't know for sure."

Amanda removed the recipe card from its box and handed it to Kari. "Here, I have an extra copy. Remember to poke the holes in the sheet cake while it's still hot; then pour in the gelatin and let it set."

"Yeah, thanks." Kari tried to focus her eyes on the recipe, but the words insisted on swimming across the surface of the card.

"Hey, come on, kid. Hang in there. Remember, 'In all thy ways. . . . ' "

Kari reached out and took her friend's hand and smiled. "I'm sorry I'm such a sad sack tonight, but enough is enough!"

Kari looked forward to her weekly visits with Amanda, and always, she dreaded returning to her mother's flat. "I'll never be able to think of the place as home again," she sighed.

During the week that followed, Kari received the promised invitation and immediately wrote that she'd be delighted to come. The weeks passed quickly, yet agonizingly slow for Kari as she both apartment hunted and prepared for her trip to Wisconsin.

On the morning she was to leave, Kari bustled about her mother's apartment, preparing food that would keep until Thanksgiving Day. She packed her luggage and added the last-minute touch-ups to every room. Marc would arrive momentarily, and she'd decided that everything must be perfect. She stood back surveying her efforts. The beer stains on the couch had been impossible to remove, but barely showed with strategically located throw pillows strewn about. The broken spring in the overstuffed chair was hidden beneath a brightly colored afghan Kari had just finished crocheting the night before. She knew, compared to his home, that it didn't measure up.

"Like it or lump it, it's the best I can do," she decided and returned to the kitchen to remove the pumpkin pies from the oven. Long ago Kari had noticed that when there was work to be done, both her mom and Keith managed to be absent, usually at the corner pub. But she had to admit she preferred it that way.

She heard them enter the building two flights down. Obvious, by Keith's cursing and Sheena's giggles, they were both decidedly drunk. Kari sighed, took off the blue gingham apron, and laid it on the table. She'd need to put her mother to bed before the woman passed out on the living room floor. And somehow she would convince Keith to make another trip to the bar down the street.

"Lord, You know how I want everything to be perfect when Marc arrives. Please help me," Kari whispered as she opened the apartment door.

"Here, Keith, let me help you with Mom." She took the staggering woman from his grasp and led her into the master bedroom. After she tucked the drunken woman beneath the clean, cool sheets, Kari gathered up her mother's soiled clothes and took them to the washing machine on the back porch. Keith stood glowering by the sink when she reentered the kitchen, standing between her and the hall leading to the other room. The evil gleam in his eye told her that she was in for trouble.

"Hey, baby, gonna tuck your papa into bed too, like you did your mama?" Keith sneered.

"You are *not* my father. Now please move. I have a lot to do before I leave for Wisconsin," she ordered as matter-of-factly as she could. Inside, Kari didn't feel nearly as strong as her tone implied, and under her breath, she prayed, "Lord, help me. Please *help me*."

"Hee, hee," Keith snickered, "Mama can't help you this time, and you can't hide behind that little old lock on your bedroom door, either. I took it off last night while you were at work. Didn't you notice?" Her heart sank as he dangled the bolt lock before her eyes. "Come on, lovey. Don't be such a cold fish. Forget your religion for a few minutes and have some fun," he teased, inching closer with each word.

She glanced quickly from one side to the other, searching for an escape. "Now, Keith, stop right where you are. You and Sheena have been doing much better lately. Don't blow it now."

"Hey, babe, didn't you learn last time, before you ran away to that Wisconsin farm, your mama will believe anything I tell her. Remember?" He slouched against the wall, arms folded across his chest.

Kari *did* remember. It was her mother's accusations that had hurt the most. To be accused of encouraging this monster, of luring him to her bedroom, of teasing him with her feminine wiles, had been too much. If Amanda hadn't come to her rescue, Kari didn't know what she would have done. The nightmares she'd had at the Wynters' home seemed to be coming all too true.

Kari thought she heard a familiar voice, but decided she must have been mistaken. She strained, but could hear no sound other than Keith's ragged breathing. Slowly, deliberately, Kari turned, slid the hot pads over her hands, and picked up the freshly baked pumpkin pie.

"Keith, stop this nonsense right now! Get out of my way." Her eyes flashed anger. "Do you see this pie? Straight from the oven, not five minutes ago. It would brand you for life. Now move it!"

"Why, you little wild cat!" He crouched ready to spring. "But I like my women spirited."

"I mean it, Keith. Move! Now!" She took a step forward. Instead of retreating, he doubled over in pain.

"Ooh," he groaned, clutching his stomach. "Do something. My gut aches something terrible. Ooh, ouch!"

"What? What's the matter?" She'd noticed that often after a drinking bout Keith favored his stomach. "Maybe something is seriously wrong with him," Kari thought. She turned and set the pie on the stove. Before she could turn to face him again, she felt his arms lock around hers and squeeze hard, pinning her arms straight down behind her back. She choked, terrified of the consequences of her foolish move.

"OK, sweetie," he cooed, "now the game is going to be played my way." He inched her backward toward the hall door. "We're going to go beddy-bye, just you and me."

Kari opened her mouth to scream, when suddenly she felt her body fall backward, and at the same instant she heard Keith's body hit the kitchen wall. Had he stumbled?

*"Let the lady go!"*

The familiar voice made Kari's knees weaken, almost give out from under her. At the same time she felt Keith's arms tighten around hers.

*"I said, 'Let the lady go!' "*

Keith arms released their hold, and Kari darted to the other side of the kitchen. She stared at Marc in wonder and disbelief. Marc held the cringing Keith by the nape of the neck.

"Oh, Marc," Kari choked, "how can I ever thank you?"

"Sorry about walking in without knocking, but the front door was open, and I couldn't help overhearing your conversation. Oh yes, where do you want me to deposit this creep?"

"Uh, I don't know. How about out in the hall?" Kari pointed to the front door.

"Sounds fine with me." Marc gave the drunken man another shake by the collar. "Don't come back until you're sure Kari and I are across the state line!"

Teetering on the verge of tears, Kari ran to her bedroom and yanked her suitcase across the bed. Her fingers shook as she attempted to lock it.

Here, let me help you." Marc reached for her hand and deftly snapped each lock closed. Then he turned and took Kari's arms in his hand, holding her at arm's length. "It's OK, you know. You can cry."

"Let's just get out of here, please." With Marc standing so close, it was hard to remember that a girl named Yvonne waited patiently for him to return to the university after the holidays. Kari whirled about and picked up her sports bag. "I'm ready."

"Do you have everything? Everything you'd need if you decided not to come back?" Marc asked.

"Well, no." Kari tipped her head questioningly. "But really I don't—"

"Then get with it. I have no intention of allowing you to return. I'm sure when Mom and Dad hear about this, they will say the same thing."

"Allowing? You're doing it again!" Kari's hackles rose in defense.

Marc looked surprised. "Doing what?"

"Bullying me! Trying to tell me what to do. I appreciate your help and your concern, but I'm an adult. I have to make my own decisions." She rubbed her arms as if warding off an unexplained chill. "Oh, I don't know. I have a good job here in the city. I can't just go traipsing off to the north woods with you or anyone else."

Marc flung his arms defensively into the air. "Hey look, I'm sorry for being so bossy, but I care about you. Can't you see that? I don't want to let that creep within a hundred miles of you." He stopped, stared at the ceiling for a few seconds, and heaved a deep sigh. A moment later he turned back to her. "Right now, if it's all right with you, let's just pack everything that's important to you and get out of here." Marc grinned, and his blue eyes twinkled teasingly. "We *do* have hospitals up in the north woods, as you call it. Where you got that term from, I'll never know."

"I'm sorry. You're right, of course. I— can't come back to this place. And I'd planned to get my own place after the holidays anyway. Now it looks like I have no choice." She skipped across the room to the closet and lifted a small wooden box from the shelf. "I have some money saved for a deposit and for the first month's rent. Let me get it before we leave."

She opened the box and gasped. It was empty! Someone had removed every dollar she'd saved for the last three months. Kari dropped to the edge of the bed. Nothing could stop her tears this time. Her plans lay in shambles before the one person she'd hoped to impress the most. Everything had gone wrong, terribly wrong.

Compassion flooded Marc's face as he sat down beside her. His strong arms engulfed her. "Come on, let's just get out of here."

Defeat swept through Kari. "I . . . I . . . I would like to write a note to my mother before I go, to tell her goodbye," she whispered.

A few minutes later, when Kari and Marc emerged from the large brownstone apartment house, Keith was nowhere to be seen. They rode in silence to Amanda's apartment. Kari stayed in the car while Marc went inside.

Immediately sensing that something had happened, Amanda rushed the children into the car. The 175-mile trip to the farm was silent except for the children's exuberance at visiting Uncle Marcus and Aunt Ruth.

Later that night, when Mom Wynters came into Kari's room, ostensibly with extra blankets, Kari broke. "I tried so hard," she wept. "I really believed that God wanted me to help Sheena find the Saviour. Instead, I'm forced to leave while she's in a drunken stupor. I even tried to like Keith for my mom's sake. I really tried. And for a time, I thought maybe I was getting through." She paused and looked Mom full in the face. "Why? Why does everything go so wrong?" she whispered.

"At times it seems that way, I'll admit," Mom said. "And it's easy to quote promises like 'All things work together for good for them that love God.' However, it's more difficult to claim such promises in the midst of trouble. But then, what else is there but God and His Word?" Mom smoothed a heavy red woolen blanket over the comforter.

"Kari," she continued, "maybe I should have tried harder to discourage you from returning home last September." Mom paused and ran the blanket's satin binding between her fingers. "More than ever, I want you to stay here, with us. I'll beg, tease, cajole—but of course you must do what you believe God wants you to do. As you said, you do have responsibilities at the hospital where you work."

"That's not entirely true, Mom. My job at the hospital will end on January first, and as yet I haven't located another to take its place." Kari sighed.

Mom's face darkened, and she bit her lip nervously. "I have an apology to make. I did something I shouldn't have even before I knew of your problem. I scheduled a tentative job interview for you at the Beaver Dam Community Hospital. It's no problem if you want to cancel it. I'll understand. Dad had fits, said I was putting too much pressure on you. But, well, they need nurses desperately. And now, with this happening, you will at least consider it, won't you?"

Kari kissed the woman's cheek. "Sure, I'll consider it."

Mom gave Kari a quick squeeze. "And you don't need to worry about Marc. He'll be back at the university until late spring."

"Marc? How did he get into this discussion?" Kari fumbled with her covers.

"I'm a mother, and I'm not blind." The older woman smiled and reached for the light switch. "See you bright and early. We can talk more then. And oh, yes, did I tell you that it's so good to have you home again, Kari?"

# Chapter 11
# Yvonne

Sitting in the pew between Mindy and Mom Wynters during the special Thanksgiving services at church, Kari decided to completely block out the ugliness she'd left behind in Chicago. Later, somewhere between the cranberry sauce and the pumpkin pie, she suddenly realized that she felt completely happy for the first time since she'd left the farm at the end of August.

Thanksgiving afternoon Marc suggested he and Kari drive over to see Grandma Lewis. Grandma met them at the door. "Come in. You're letting in the cold. I just can't wait to tell you about the plan I have to keep Kari here in Wisconsin." She looked at Kari with a twinkle in her eyes. "Kari, since you feel that you would be burdening the Wynters by staying with them, I'd like to ask you to stay with me. I could really use your company."

Grandma continued, her face lit up like a ten-years-old's. "I understand you will probably work nights, but it would be great knowing that someone was around most of the time to help me if I needed it.

"Also, I got to thinking that you'll need a car to get to and from the hospital. And well, old Ginny's just sitting out there in the barn going to rust. She's a mighty purty beast when she's been shined up." Grandma paused, giving Kari time to answer.

Kari shook her head in amazement.

"That is, if you could stand living with a crotchety old woman. I'd love having you here." A hopeful little smile touched Grandma's face as she reached out to grasp Kari's hand.

Kari looked to Marc, then back at Grandma Lewis. "I—I don't know what to say. What do you think, Marc?

"Well," Marc paused, stroking his chin, "I don't want to be accused of being bossy or anything, but Mom would worry less, knowing someone was here with Gram, especially during the winter months."

Kari pursed her lips thoughtfully. "We could at least give it a try, I

64

suppose, if we could work out a fair financial agreement for room and board— and, of course, a fair price for the car."

Grandma raised her hand to object. "No, no. I wouldn't want you to pay me for anything. Just having you with me will be payment enough for your room and the little you eat. And as to the car, I stopped driving last fall when my driver's license expired. My eyes are getting weak."

"Either I pay my way, or I won't do it." The muscles in Kari's chin tightened stubbornly.

"Give in, Gram. She's as bullheaded as you. I'll tell you what. I'll be glad to give the old Chevy a checkup and get it running smoothly again." Marc ambled to the sofa and sat down. For a moment the two women silently challenged one another. Marc leaned back on the sofa, grinning at the sight of Grandma Lewis being outmaneuvered for a change.

"What's the car worth, Marc?" Kari lifted her chin in defiance.

"I dunno. A '68 Chev? I'd say $500 maybe. I know the Chevy dealer in town, and I'm sure he's home today. I'll call and find out," Marc drawled, and he reached for the phone.

"Now, Kari Gerard, you know that you don't have that kind of money," Grandma began.

Sensing a hint of defeat in Grandma's voice, Kari took advantage of the moment. "I will if you agree to let me pay for the car over a ten-month-period, say." She paused and waited. "Well? Do you agree to my terms? Do I pay you a fair price for the car and for my room and board, or do I look elsewhere?"

"Hmmph!" the old woman sniffed. "These younguns these days have no respect for age and wisdom!" A tiny grin played at the corners of her mouth.

"But only until summer," Kari said, shooting a dark glance at Marc. "I know how much you treasure your privacy. And I know why you're doing this. I see Marc's fingerprints all over this entire scheme. Right?" Kari's dark eyes bored into Marc's clear blue eyes. He shrugged his shoulders and waved his hands in innocence.

"I want you to stay with me. Him?" She snorted. "He doesn't count! And as for summer, let's wait and see what happens by then, OK? It's a long way off. Now, how about a nice hot cup of herbal tea? I have cinnamon-orange, kaffir, and peppermint. Which would you like?"

"We'll be over tomorrow to move her in," Marc assured her. "Mindy and Amanda already agreed to help. Oops." He clapped a hand over his mouth. "I think I just goofed." His face reddened at Grandma's glare.

"Tsk! tsk! Now if you'll just remove your feet long enough to enjoy your tea and cookies, Marc." Grandma nodded her head graciously and smiled.

On the way back to the Wynters place Kari decided it was time she and Marc had a little talk. "Mark, I as I told you before, I appreciate your concern, and I am eternally in your debt for your help the other day with Keith, but I don't appreciate your trying to regulate my life."

"Kari, I was only trying to help," Marc mumbled, contrite.

"I realize that. Last summer it was different, but you have Yvonne to think about now. Bully her if you can." Kari's left foot tapped out her anger on the truck's floorboard. Kari sensed that Marc was close to the boiling point.

She hastened on. "I am going to have to make my own decisions. Please, you will always be very special to me, but you can't run my life." She emphasized the word *can't*.

Marc answered in a low, steady tone. "Sometimes you make me so angry, Kari Gerard."

Marc drove on in silence. She gazed at him out of the corner of her eye. He was everything she wanted in a man—nothing like Keith. That day in the apartment, with Marc glaring and Keith cringing, Kari hadn't had time to think. But in the days since, she'd come to realize that Marc was everything Keith wasn't—that she'd been unfair to lump all men into one category—lecherous. Yet Marc's aggressiveness frightened her. Whether it was an urge to control her or to protect her didn't really matter. If she'd learned anything during the last few years, it was to be her own person. "Marc will need to accept that if he intends to be my friend or—" She stopped her thought midsentence and shook her head sadly. "Or what?"

As they pulled into the driveway, Marc broke the silence between them. "But you know I'm right. Moving in with Gram is your best move right now since you seem to think you'd be sponging off the folks if you lived at the house. They don't agree, I might add."

"Marc, it's OK. Just don't do it again." Kari wrapped her coat tightly about her and stared out the car window.

"I don't understand you at all. I try to—"

Kari laughed and shook her head. "Isn't that the lament of most men, not understanding women?"

"Hmmph!" A dimple teased at the corner of his mouth. "You've got all the answers, don't you?"

"No, but I'm working on it," she replied.

"Friends?"

"Friends," she agreed.

Marc left for school early Monday morning, taking Amanda and her two children with him. With the routine of her new job to learn and studying for and passing the state licensing exam, Kari found that the weeks between Thanksgiving and Christmas passed quickly. Mindy dropped by Grandma's house every day after school to see Kari. Kari could tell that Grandma appreciated having someone to talk to. And she basked in the love the Wynters family and Grandma Lewis again bestowed upon her.

Though nothing had been mentioned about Yvonne and the pending engagement, Kari dreaded the day Marc would return home for Christmas vacation with the news. Three days before his scheduled return, Mindy arrived at Grandma's house, her face drawn, her eyes red. Kari had just finished her late-afternoon breakfast and was sitting in the kitchen regaling Grandma with the most recent happenings at the small-town hospital when Mindy burst through the front door. "Oh, Kari, the worst thing has happened!" she cried as she ran into the kitchen.

Kari rushed to the girl's side. "Mindy, what's wrong? Has someone been hurt?"

"Mama got a letter from Marc, and he's gone and gotten himself engaged to that dumb Yvonne. I hate her!" Mindy shouted defiantly, stamping her foot.

Grandma jumped to the maligned girl's defense. "Hey, hey now. You don't even know the poor girl. She might be very nice. Take off your ski jacket, and tell us all about it."

Kari stood silently by the kitchen table, speechless, while Mindy blurted the news of Marc's engagement.

"She's supposed to be very rich, lives over near Detroit somewhere. How could he? How could he ask her to marry him? She can't love him anywhere near as much as you do, Kari," Mindy wailed.

Kari's face blanched. "Out of the mouths of babes," she thought. She cleared her throat. Her mouth went dry. Stumbling to the sink she reached for a tumbler to get a drink of water. She turned on the faucet and leaned over the sink in pain as the icy tap water ran into the glass.

"How is this possible, Lord? Didn't You promise that all things work together . . . ? Is this Your plan for Marc, for me?"

All the joy of the Christmas season drained out of Kari in the days that followed. She went through the motions of buying and wrapping gifts for her adopted family. At night, while her patients slept, she searched God's Word for assurance that He was still guiding her. She prayed for relief from the anger that she harbored toward Marc, and release from the vicious jealousy toward Yvonne that she felt building inside her. "Lord, when Yvonne comes to visit, help me to demonstrate Your love. Help me to be kind." Kari memorized promise after promise as ammunition against Yvonne's arrival.

By Christmas Eve, as she and Grandma drove through a snowstorm on their way to the Wynters' place, Kari realized that she was more or less at peace with the situation and with God. She wasn't sure how she'd feel when she actually met Yvonne, but she decided to give it all she had.

The presence of the soft, pale, fluffy blonde on Marc's arm didn't unnerve her as much as she'd imagined it would. Kari smiled a wry grin as Yvonne's bubbly, innocent expression turned to distrust when they were introduced. From that moment, Kari knew she'd survive, she'd go on. "And by hook or by crook," she determined, "I'll wish Marc and his bride-to-be, the very best."

The Wynters' house seemed about to burst with people and happiness that evening. Kari especially enjoyed finally getting to meet Marc's older sister, Shelly, and her husband. When the entire family gathered around the Christmas tree for Dad's annual reading of the Christmas story, Kari realized that even with Marc in the arms of another, her own place in the Wynters' family was secure.

As she drove to work later that night, Kari had time to think. She kept fighting a disquieting concern for Marc and Yvonne's relationship. Somehow Marc didn't appear as happy as a newly betrothed fiancé should. His usual banter and good humor seemed to be missing.

Kari thought about Yvonne. No matter how she tried, Kari just couldn't handle much more of the girl's helplessness. "Marky do this. Marky do that. Marky, I'm cold. Marky, I'm thirsty. Marky! Marky! Marky! How can he stand it?" She banged the steering wheel with her palms. "Maybe I should just chalk it all up to jealousy," she decided. "I'm probably searching for things *not* to like about Yvonne."

Kari parked the car in the employee's parking area and dashed through the accumulating snow into the hospital. "Sorry, Lord, I'm regressing, I'm afraid, with this jealousy thing. I still have a long way to go, I guess." Kari rushed to her floor, hung her ski jacket in the nurses' lounge, and hurried to the nursing station. Kari had arranged to work most of the Christmas holiday on purpose. And now, Christmas Eve or otherwise, her shift had begun.

Around 3:00 a.m. Kari glanced up from the patients' charts to notice that the elevator had stopped at her floor. When the doors opened, Marc strolled out. "Hi," he drawled. A grin the size of Lake Michigan filled his face.

"What are *you* doing *here*? At *this* hour?" Kari asked anxiously. "Is everyone all right?"

"Fine, far as I know. So how are you doing? I haven't seen much of you this vacation." Marc grabbed an empty wheelchair and made himself comfortable.

"Marc, you can't be up here on the floors at this hour of the night."

"Yes I can. Dr. Ripley is on duty downstairs, and he gave me permission to stay for thirty minutes or until you got busy—whichever came first. This is small town USA, remember? And if you know the right people—" Unaffected, he ran his left pinkie fingernail under his right hand nails.

With a flair worthy of a Hollywood Oscar Nominee, Kari whipped opened one of the metal chart holders and began to write. "Well, I am busy, as you can see. I must get the charts up to date before my relief comes on duty."

"You have four hours in which to complete that task. You didn't know I worked one school year as an orderly here in this very hospital, did you? You can't fool me." He twirled the wheelchair in a circle on two wheels.

Kari scoffed at his demonstration. "Showoff!"

Marc wheeled up to the desk and placed his chin on his folded arms and stared into her eyes. "Tell me the truth. I respect your judgment. What do you think of Yvonne?"

"Umm, she's very pretty—has a lovely smile—she seems to think the world of you." Kari cleared her throat, searching for something more to say. "Besides, why are you asking me? She's your fiancée. You must have thought all this out before you asked her to marry you."

"Well, it was your fault really. After our disagreement during Thanksgiving vacation I decided that perhaps Yvonne's dependence would be a real asset in a wife. I guess I decided that I want a woman that needs me." He paused. "That sounds sort of chauvinistic, doesn't it?"

"You said it, I didn't," Kari mumbled under her breath.

"Pardon?"

"Just agreeing with you. First of all, don't blame me for the choices you make, dear friend. I have enough burdens of my own to carry. And another choice tidbit, remember the old adage about judging a book by its cover."

"What do you mean by that remark?" Marc scowled.

"I don't know, probably nothing. Just don't make a serious decision like this hastily. Be sure it's the way God would have you go." Kari paused and pursed her lips. "Seems to me that a mature, lasting relationship needs time, you know, to become friends as well as lovers. Grandma always says, 'Winter 'em and summer 'em before you marry 'em.' "

Kari stopped and laughed. "Don't I sound like the ancient seer, passing out sage advice to the young?" She glanced across the desk into Marc's piercing blue eyes, intending to laugh again. Instead, his gaze disarmed her. She caught her breath, but determined not to be the first to look away this time. He stared into her eyes for several seconds. Though neither uttered a word, a flood of meaningful communication passed between them.

Suddenly, Marc stood up and wheeled the chair back to where he had found it. "Well, I'd better be getting on home. Dad and Michael will be heading out to the barn to do morning chores. I'm sure they'd appreciate my help."

He strolled to the elevator and pushed the call button. "Thanks, thanks a lot for the advice. You know, you're one special lady. And thanks for giving Yvonne a chance. You could have made things pretty rough for her last night, but you didn't. She's really a very nice person, you know."

"I'm sure she is. She definitely has good taste in men," Kari added, her eyes twinkling as Marc blushed and jumped into the elevator a scant second before the doors closed.

"Ooh!" Kari took a deep breath. For several minutes she tapped a pencil point absently on the desk top, mulling over Marc's true motives for his unexpected visit, and her own definite response. "How strange," she thought, "to feel the closest to Marc at a time when I'm giving him advice about another woman."

# Chapter 12
# Grace Under Pressure

On Christmas Day Kari drove into the Wynters' driveway and hurried up the walk. Even before she reached the front steps, she could hear the ebullient strains of "Joy to the World" drifting out of the living room. Through the large picture window she watched the family, except for Marc and Yvonne, gathered around the old upright piano, singing carols. "Ooh! I just love Christmas!" she exclaimed as she stomped the snow off her boots and burst inside.

"Hi everybody," she called.

Shelly and Dad beckoned her to join them. As she entered the room, she noticed Marc and Yvonne sitting in the dining room, Marc's face drawn and distressed, Yvonne's in a pout. "Hmmph," she thought, "trouble in paradise?" Quickly, she glanced heavenward. "I didn't really wish such a thing, Lord. Honest."

After everyone tired of singing, Dad brought out the family slides. "Sorry, Kari, but this is a Christmas tradition around here. You'll have to endure it, I'm afraid."

"Sounds good to me," she said, plunking herself down on the carpet beside Mindy.

Dad placed a tray of slides on the machine. "OK, turn off the lights. Here we go."

Everyone was laughing at a picture of Marc and Shelly making mud pies when Yvonne stormed through the room and up the stairs. The laughter suddenly died. Even the younger children looked uncomfortably at one another.

Kari turned to see Marc. He stood with his arms crossed, leaning defiantly against the living room wall, staring straight ahead at the screen. No one spoke as Dad clicked a number of slides through the projector.

Finally Mom cleared her throat. "Marc, should I go upstairs to Yvonne? She's a guest in my home, you know."

"Do whatever you want, Mom. But I want to see these pictures, espe-

70

cially the ones of Shelly trying to feed the mud pies to baby Michael."

Michael reared up from where he'd been lying on the floor. "Hey, watch who you're calling baby, big brother," he teased, knowing he was almost eye to eye with Marc now.

Marc dropped to the floor laughing. "All right. You win, tough guy."

Mom headed upstairs to Yvonne while everyone else continued enjoying the slides.

Kari drove home after the slides were finished. She was glad to have the night off from work. Maybe she could get some extra sleep. She tiptoed into the house and up to her room so as not to waken Grandma.

Early the next morning, long before Kari had planned to get up, the phone rang. She groaned but went to answer it.

"Hello," she yawned and scratched the back of her head.

"Kari? This is Mindy. We're going skating down at Beaver Dam, on the lake. Ya wanna come with us?"

Kari gulped. Ice skating? She'd not gone ice skating since she was ten years old. "Oh, I don't know."

"Aw, come on. Everyone's going. Well, all of us kids, that is. Mom and Dad are going to babysit."

"Kids?"

"Yeah, me and Aunt Amanda, Michael, Marc and his fiancée . . ."

"Mindy!" Kari threatened.

Mindy paused dramatically, then sighed. "OK, Marc and Yvonne, and Shelly and John."

"All right, I'll come if you have a decent pair of skates that will fit me," Kari answered, immediately regretting her hasty decision. "I'll break my neck for sure," she warned.

"No you won't. You'll do just fine," Mindy assured her. "We'll pick you up in half an hour."

Kari hurried around the house, digging out her heaviest clothes. Grandma Lewis soon caught the spirit by supplying her with a fast breakfast. By the time one of the cars pulled into the driveway, Kari felt more like the abominable snowman than a person. Mindy threw open the car door, gesturing Kari into the back seat beside her. Michael and Amanda were in the front. Michael was driving.

Amanda turned around toward Kari. "We're meeting the rest down at the lake. Michael wanted to show off his brand new driver's license."

"Good going, Michael! You didn't tell me," Kari said. She patted his shoulder. He blushed and pulled out of Grandma's driveway onto the highway.

Reaching the lake, everyone piled out of the car and put on his skates. The other car arrived a few minutes later. Kari knew immediately, by Yvonne's face, that last night's problems had been resolved. As they walked toward the frozen lake, Yvonne gazed adoringly up into Marc's eyes. He looked around uncomfortably. Kari turned away and skated onto the ice before he noticed her watching.

The lake shone like crystal as the skaters skimmed across the ice. Mountains of snow had been bulldozed into massive snowbanks by the town's Department of Roads. Mindy skated up behind her. "Hey, I thought you couldn't skate."

Kari looked surprised. "I never said that."

"It's OK," Mindy giggled. "Better than OK by the looks of things."

Kari followed Mindy's gaze toward shore where Marc was leading Yvonne carefully out onto the ice. The girl squealed and screeched with every step.

"Oh dear, she doesn't know how to skate?"

Mindy shrugged her shoulders.

Kari skated to the far end of the plowed surface. Slowly, the moves she'd learned as a child returned. She decided it was fun, except for the sore ankles. A hand on her waist and another on her arm startled her.

"Hi." Michael grasped her hand and eased gracefully into Kari's stride. "You skate real well."

"Thanks, but I am a bit rusty." Kari leaned into the rhythm.

"Did you take lessons somewhere?"

"At the Y when I was a kid, but it's coming back."

Weaving back and forth between the other skaters, he whirled her about the ice like a dancing doll on a music box. She loved it.

"Michael, I've intended to ask you, have you found your blue-eyed blonde yet?" Kari teased.

"Sort of, though she's not blond and her eyes are brown." He blushed and twirled her about in a sweeping figure eight.

"Oh?"

"At least I'm working on it," he hedged, his dimples deepening.

Kari glanced toward shore, only to see Yvonne scream and grab for Marc, causing them both to fall on the ice. She watched as Marc led Yvonne to the wooden bench beside the lake. By the scowl on Yvonne's face, Kari could tell that things weren't going too well between the couple. The girl looked so despondent when Marc skated off without her that Kari's heart was touched.

"OK, Lord," she thought, "You're making me put my money where my mouth is, aren't You? I'm not sure that my compassion will go that far." She and Michael glided into another turn.

"Looks like Marc gave up on Yvonne, at least as far as ice skating is concerned," Michael drawled.

"The poor girl," Kari said sympathetically. "Excuse me, Michael, I think I can help her." She released herself from Michael's hands and sped across the ice toward Yvonne.

"Hi, Yvonne. I thought I'd come over and retie my skates. They tend to work themselves lose, and I need them tied as tight as possible to save my poor ankles." Kari sat down on the bench beside Yvonne and proceeded to tighten her skates. "The secret is in the ties, definitely!" Kari rattled on. "Would you like me to help you with yours? I'm sure they've loosened since Marc tied them for you."

The girl eyed her suspiciously. "Yeah, I guess so."

As Kari retied the skates she talked on, about her life in Wisconsin, about her skating lessons, about anything that would bridge the gap between them. "Now, here, let me help you up." She grabbed Yvonne's hands.

"No, I don't want to make a further fool of myself. Besides, I feel stupid in this outfit. Look at me! I look more like an old farmer than anything else." Yvonne blushed when it dawned on her what she had said.

Kari ignored the comment and pulled Yvonne to her feet. "Come on; it's easy. You can do it. As to falling, we all do it."

Right on cue, Mindy took a tumble, landing firmly on her backside. Kari burst out laughing. "See, what did I tell you? And look, there go Shelly and John." Kari smiled at the fortunate timing of everyone's falls.

Slowly, almost without Yvonne realizing it, Kari led the girl onto the ice. "Now, see? Put your feet like this, placing your weight on your left foot. Then push off with your right. Good. That's good! Now one after the other, push and glide, push and glide. You've got it!"

Yvonne panicked as Kari released one of her hands. "Don't let go of me."

"I'm right here. It's OK." Kari slipped her free hand under Yvonne's elbow and guided her around the ice. Before long Yvonne felt confident enough to skate alone. Kari smiled in spite of her mixed emotions when Marc skated up to Yvonne and suggested a couple skate.

As she watched them disappear behind a six-foot snow pile, Amanda and the rest of the group skated up behind her. "Come on, Kari, we're going to crack the whip, and you get to be on the end." Amanda's eyes told her that the suggestion had been carefully timed.

"Sure, why not?" Kari grabbed hold of Mindy's hand and dug her skates into the ice as they raced to the far end of the lake.

On the way home in the car, Mindy looked across the car seat at Kari and asked, "Why did you do it? Help Yvonne I mean."

Kari smiled and searched for the words that would help Mindy to understand. "Yvonne is having a rough time fitting into your family, isn't she?"

Mindy nodded her head.

"That's the reason. You are a terrific family. I love every one of you; but together, you can be mighty intimidating. Especially the love—it's overwhelming to those of us who aren't accustomed to it."

Mindy wrinkled her nose. "So you felt sorry for her."

"Partly," Kari admitted.

"But you love Marc. I know you do." Mindy sounded accusing.

"Yes, and it's because I care that I want to make it easy for him and for Yvonne." Kari gazed in Mindy's troubled eyes. "Do you understand?"

"Yeah, I guess." Mindy dropped her head and stared out the window. "Mom would call it grace under pressure, or something like that."

Kari shook her head. "Hardly, Mindy."

Mindy tightened her lips, forming a thin, stubborn line. "I don't care. I still don't like her."

Kari reached across the seat and patted Mindy's gloved hand. "You're just biased. And right or wrong, I love you for it."

When they reached the turnoff for Grandma's place, Michael drove on by. Kari suggested that he missed the turn, but Amanda informed her that Grandma was already at the Wynters' place with a change of clothes for her and that Mom had supper waiting. "If you really want to go back home, Michael will take you, of course. Do you have to work tonight?" Amanda asked.

"That's OK," Kari groaned. "I'm supposed to work tonight, but I'm not sure my body can take the strain. I am hurting in places I didn't even know existed this morning."

Amanda laughed and agreed. "It's been a mighty long time since I last skated, and it will be a mighty long time before I do it again!"

As Michael swung the car into the driveway, he glanced over at his aunt. "You women! Getting old before your time."

Kari swatted his shoulder playfully. "I resent that. Old before my time, indeed!"

Within minutes, all of the skaters tumbled into the house, laughing, hungry, and all talking at once. Mom and Dad Wynters listened to each tale, laughing at the falls, enjoying the adventure as much as if they'd gone along.

"Has the storm moved in yet?" Dad peered out the window into the darkness.

"I think it's starting," Marc said as he headed for the stairs. "I'll be down in a minute to help with the chores, Dad. Come on, sport," he called to Michael. "There's milking to be done."

While Grandma kept the children entertained in the family room with her tall tales, the rest of the women gathered in the kitchen to help Mom Wynters finish preparing supper. Kari took a head of leaf lettuce from the refrigerator and dropped it into the sink. Yvonne strolled over and smiled. "Here, let me help you," she volunteered.

"Sure. Be careful, though. Some of these darker leaves have tiny black bugs on them. Get them all or we'll add extra protein to the menu tonight," she warned, laughing at her joke.

Horrified, Yvonne backed away from the sink, her face drained of color. "Bugs? In the lettuce? You're joking, of course."

Kari swallowed the temptation to laugh and turned around to assure Yvonne that it was quite normal to find bugs in lettuce, and that in any event the insects would not hurt her. Mindy and Shelly covered their mouths with their hands as she spoke, and dashed from the room. Amanda and Mom Wynters continued setting the table as if they'd not heard a word of the conversation.

After everyone finished eating, Dad gathered the family into the parlor around the fireplace for worship. The room echoed and reechoed from the hymns they sang together. Kari stared out the window at the snow accumulating in the driveway as Dad read from the Bible. She could feel the love flowing about the room. She felt warmed inside and out. When Dad prayed, he mentioned each person individually. Kari liked that.

The end of his prayer signaled the beginning of a hug session for each of the children. Kari no longer held back from the group as she'd done the previous summer. She went out of her way to include Yvonne and make the girl comfortable with this delightful, yet unnerving Wynters ritual.

After prayer Mindy invited Yvonne to her room to see her doll collection. Amanda squired her children to bed. Grandma went into the family room to lie down. And Michael, John, and Marc set about assembling Sammy's Christmas tricycle while Dad sat down to read the newspaper.

Quietly, Mom motioned for Kari to follow her into the kitchen. "Kari, Grandma's feeling poorly tonight, and with this snowstorm brewing, do you think it would be wise for her to stay at the house alone?"

"No, of course not," Kari answered. "I think she's been feeling a lot worse than she lets on."

Mom agreed. "I think so too. Well, I'll try to convince her to stay over. I'll call you if I need help."

Kari returned to the living room. Dad looked up from the paper he was reading. "Kari, do you have chains? Will you be able to get through to the hospital tonight? It's getting slick out there."

"I have snow tires; won't they do?" Kari asked.

"Not in that stuff." He motioned toward the window. "Maybe you'd better call in tonight. I haven't heard a snow plow go by on the main road for the last two hours. That means either the snows are so bad that they've given up or the snow has stopped, and obviously it's not the latter."

Kari scowled, wondering what might be the best thing to do. "I wouldn't hesitate for a moment except I know they're short of nursing staff right now. We have two out on maternity leave, Ann's sick with the flu, and three others from pediatrics have been absent all week. We're already stretched beyond our limits."

Marc looked up from the assembling directions. "Dad, I'll drive her in the pickup and go get her in the morning. The pickup has chains."

"No, that's OK. I'm sure I can manage alone." Kari looked first to Marc, then to Dad.

Marc bristled, then pulled back and smiled. "It's up to you. I'd be happy to do it, and I'm sure it would save on the wear and tear of everybody's nerves if you weren't out on the roads alone, but far be it from me to tell you what to do."

Dad looked questioningly at each of them, then ducked behind his newspaper. Marc picked up the assembly plans and said, "Let me know what you decide."

Kari had to admit that when Marc first began talking she'd flared up, but she had to fight back the urge to laugh when he changed so abruptly. "You're right, Marc. I've had very little experience driving in the snow. I would appreciate it if you'd drive me to work."

Marc unwound his long legs and rose slowly to his feet. "Well, we'd better leave soon. It will take at least twice as long to get there in this storm."

"You'd better take along a thermos of hot broth or something in case you get stuck in a snow bank," Dad suggested, laying his paper down on the couch beside him. "I'll go find your mother while you two get ready."

Within fifteen minutes Marc and Kari were on their way. Kari detected a note of jealousy in Yvonne's face before they left—not that she faulted the girl one bit. She wouldn't like watching her fiancé drive off with another woman on a night like this.

"I'll need to stop by for my uniform," Kari reminded.

Marc shook his head. "Don't you have any extras at the hospital? If I drive down that road, we'll spend the night there."

Kari gulped. "I'm sure one of the nurses has an extra uniform in her locker."

As they drove along, Kari felt sure that the flakes were growing bigger and falling faster by the minute. The snow pelting the windshield made her feel like she was staring into an eerily lighted tunnel. The truck slowed until she was certain they weren't going much over ten miles an hour.

Kari glanced toward Marc. Even in the dark she could see lines of exhaustion etched deeply in his face. "I really appreciate this, Marc," she said. "You've had such a long day. You must be worn out."

"We're all tired tonight." He looked over at her and smiled. "By the way, have I ever told you how really terrific I think you are?"

"What brought that on?"

"You have bent over backward to make Yvonne feel at home. The skating, the family worship, even cajoling Mindy into civility. I really appreciate it." He reached over and squeezed her hand. "You're a one-in-a-million friend."

Kari closed her eyes and turned away, remembering Mindy's statement in the car about grace under pressure.

"Only through your power, Lord," she whispered.

# Chapter 13
# Promise of Spring

Kari sat bleary-eyed at the nursing station throughout the night. She struggled to keep her eyes open. She'd already checked her patients three times as often during the night as was customary. She'd scrubbed the kitchenette, straightened the linen closet twice, and reorganized the desk and files at least four times. The night seemed interminable.

Morning did come, however, and with it sunshine. The snowstorm had passed. A world of white dazzled her eyes as she stepped out into the sunshine. Kari felt strangely insulated from the usual sounds of the morning. She spied Marc by the side of the pickup and waved, trudging through the snow to his side.

"Have a good sleep?" she asked.

"I've had better," he groaned.

They climbed into the truck and drove to Grandma Lewis's. Though Kari didn't see Marc again before he and Yvonne returned to the university, she thought of him constantly. When Grandma returned to the house, life slipped back into a regular pattern. The new year arrived, and the month of January disappeared.

Occasionally, various young men who worked at the hospital asked Kari out for a date, but except for one concert in Madison with a medical intern, she demurred. Analyzing her reluctance, she realized that it was no longer due to Keith's influence, but because no one seemed to measure up to Marc.

Winter's bluster continued through the month of April. Then suddenly, without warning, spring arrived. Blossoming redbud trees lined the streets in town. Flowering shrubbery decorated the landscape. Daffodils, and tulips raced each other to be the first to show off for the new season. Grandma Lewis had become frail during the long winter months. She used her cane more often to get around and complained about her arthritis more. Her daughter Julia, who lived in southern Ohio, wrote weekly, begging her mother to give up the homestead and move south to live with her. Kari encouraged Grandma Lewis to accept. Reluctantly, Grandma agreed.

The day she was to leave the woman looked around the living room stacked with cardboard boxes. "You know, child," she said, glancing at Kari with red eyes, "the Wynters have been a part of my life for so long I feel that I'm actually leaving my real family behind." She paused. "And what will ever become of you?"

Kari squeezed the old woman's hand. "Now, don't start again. I'm young. I'm strong. And I have a God leading me who can produce miracles! Along with a 1968 Chevy to get me where I need to go. So stop worrying." Kari leaned forward, her forehead tenderly touching Grandma's. "You've helped me so much. And now, you're helping me more by letting me stay in this house until it sells. What more can anyone ask for?"

"If only our thick-headed Marc would wake up and dump that harpy!" Grandma sputtered. "You will let me know if anything changes in that department, won't you?"

"You'll be the first to know, I'm sure." Kari promised.

A green-and-brown paneled station wagon with out-of-state plates pulled into the yard. The middle-aged Julia hopped out of the car and ran to her mother's arms. "Oh, Mama, everyone's delighted that you're coming to live with us!"

Kari helped Julia load the boxes in the back of the car and waved as they pulled out of the driveway. Her life would change with Grandma Lewis gone, for sure. But if there was one thing Kari decided she should be accustomed to, it was change. She ambled out to the mailbox, collected the mail, and ran back to the house. "Brr! It's still heavy-sweater weather out there," she decided.

Once inside, Kari checked the stack of mail. There was an electric bill, a flyer sent out by a district councilman, an advertisement offering a special at the local pizza parlor, and a letter from Sheena, her mother. Kari still couldn't believe the changes her mother had made over the winter months. Her letters spoke of Alcoholics Anonymous meetings, of a new job as a sales clerk in an appliance store, even of occasional church attendance. "My mother? Sheena? In church?" Kari hardly dared believe it possible. Sheena's letters never mentioned Keith, and Kari never asked. "Yes, perhaps this springtime will be a new beginning for all of us," she thought as she tore open the envelope and sank into the closest arm chair. Suddenly the telephone rang. She ran to answer it.

"Hello, Kari Gerard's residence. Yes, this is Kari." She paused, and a look of alarm replaced the smile on her face. "What? When? How badly were they hurt? Yes, of course, I'll be right over. Tell them not to worry, I'll take care of everything. Yes, thank you for calling."

Kari struggled to remain calm. There'd been a car accident on Highway 33 west of Beaver Dam. Dad had swerved to miss a five-year-old boy wandering down the middle of the highway. His right wheel hit the edge of the road, and in the soft mud the car rolled. Both he and Mom had been hospitalized. They were not critical, but they had definitely been injured, and the extent of their injuries were yet unknown.

Kari grabbed the keys and hopped into her car, spinning gravel the length of the driveway. "Mindy and Michael should be getting home from school at any moment," she said to herself. "Mom is worried about them, I'm sure." As she drove, she listed all the tasks to be done. "Call Marc. Call Shelly and her husband, John, in Minneapolis. Call Amanda. Take the kids to the hospital. Get off work tonight so as to stay with the kids." Kari drove up to the house just as Mindy and Michael entered the front door.

Stunned, ashen faced, they stared at her in disbelief when she told them of the accident. Kari pulled Mindy into her arms as tears cascaded down the young girl's face. Michael fought to keep from crying.

"It's OK, Michael. It's OK to cry," Kari soothed. "Get busy," she thought, "Get busy and keep the kids busy too."

"Michael, while we drive to the hospital, could you make a list of all the people we should call? But before we place the calls I think we'd better find out how serious things are. We need to have something definite to tell everyone," Kari reasoned as they climbed back into her car.

"But the evening chores—" Michael began.

"We'll get you back in time. And when we do, Mindy and I will come down to the barn to help. Come on, car, let's go!" Kari pumped the pedal, sending too much gas through the lines. "Slow down, kiddo," she cautioned. "Haste makes waste, remember?"

At the hospital, they learned that Mom had broken her collarbone, cracked three ribs, and possibly had a concussion, while Dad had a broken leg and a mild concussion. Both had been sedated for the night. The hospital's head nurse agreed that Kari should stay with Mindy and Michael instead of reporting for work.

Kari found an empty phone booth and started calling the names on Michael's list, beginning with Marc. It took a while to locate him on campus. He'd been in the library studying. When he answered the phone, he sounded preoccupied until he recognized Kari's voice.

"Marc, this is Kari. I have some bad news. There's been an automobile accident. Everyone's safe though." She explained about the accident and the extent of his parents' injuries.

"I gotta get home tonight! Michael can't manage the milking alone," Marc answered. His voice sounded as though it had risen at least an octave. "I've got finals tomorrow, but they don't matter now—" Marc's sentence trailed off.

"Don't be silly," Kari said. "You're hundreds of miles from here. You couldn't possibly get home in time to help with the chores. It's all we're going to be able to do to make it from here."

Marc sighed. "I guess you're right."

"The three of us can manage just fine tonight and in the morning. That will give you time to make whatever arrangements you need to make at your end. Also, I'll worry less if you aren't on the road tonight, you know. We don't need another mishap." Kari scowled, tapping the wall impatiently with her fingertips. She was worried. Marc sounded so unnatural.

"That makes sense, I guess. Are you sure you three can handle it tonight? Call the Hardings next door. They'll come over and help, I'm sure," Marc suggested.

"That's a good idea. Thanks. I'd better hang up—this is costing money. Don't worry about calling the rest of your family. Michael made me a list, so I can take care of that. And, Marc, please drive carefully," Kari reminded.

"I think I'd like to call my sister, Shelly, if you don't mind."

"Fine, that will be one less call for me to make from this end. Take care now, and take it easy. Don't do anything stupid, you understand?" Kari scolded.

"Yes, Mama, I'll be careful," he laughed.

"See that you are." Kari grinned. "Seriously, do be careful. We need you here, in one piece."

"I will, I promise. Give Michael and Mindy a hug, and tell them I'll see them tomorrow sometime. Goodnight, Kari."

After the last call was completed, Kari, Mindy, and Michael drove back to the farm. Already emotionally exhausted, they changed into jeans and work shirts and headed for the barn. Even though Kari had spent a summer on the farm, she had never actually helped with the milking chores.

Michael immediately took charge, assigning tasks for each of the girls to perform. The chores took an hour longer than usual, but at last three tired, sweaty farm hands stumbled back to the house for hot showers, cookies and milk, and a good night's sleep. They knew that all too soon morning would arrive, and the process would begin again. Kari ached in places she'd never dreamed possible. "Yes, it will definitely be nice to have Marc here, for more reasons than I can count," she decided. As her pain increased, her respect for dairy farmers and the local Holstein population rose markedly.

Slowly she climbed the stairs, waving a listless goodnight to the other two as she veered toward her bedroom. When she reached the room, Kari ran her hand across the puffy comforter covering the white canopied bed. She glanced appreciatively about the space she'd learned to call home almost a year earlier. Brushing her fingers through her stringy, sweaty ponytail, she remembered how badly she needed a hot shower.

After a short but thorough shower, Kari ran and jumped in the middle of the bed. With one shake of her moist curls, her head sank into the downy pillow. She reached for the light.

Almost simultaneously, or so it seemed, the alarm on the nightstand beside the bed jarred her awake. Something must be wrong. She fumbled for the light switch. The clock said 5:00 a.m.—chore time. "I just fell asleep," she argued. She could hear Michael stumbling down the stairs to the kitchen. Kari awakened Mindy, and together they trudged back to the barn for morning chores.

As she tossed feed to the cows, she remembered Marc's suggestion that she contact the neighbor for help. Kari's sore back nagged her for not making that call. Worse yet, there'd be no hot breakfast waiting for them when they reached the house. By the time she finished delivering feed, long, moist strands of black hair stuck to her cheeks. The red scarf she'd tied around her head no longer held them in place. She wiped the sweat from her forehead, leaving a trail of grime across her brow. One particularly ornery cow kicked a mound of manure into her face, creating instant freckles.

"Oh, no," Kari wailed, wiping her hand across her face, streaking her cheeks further. A laugh from the doorway caused her to turn angrily toward the intruder. "How dare you—" she stopped and stared. "Marc, you're here!" She fought back tears of frustration and relief. Then on an impulse she straightened to her full height. "As you can see, we have everything under control." Kari tilted her nose high in the air and sauntered toward the doorway and would have been convincing had it not been for the slight limp she'd acquired during the last twelve hours. "However, if you wish to have a hot breakfast, I'll need to go up to the house and clean up a bit."

Marc cleared his throat, attempting to contain his laughter. "Everything under control?"

A warning glance from Michael didn't come soon enough to save Marc. As Kari came even with Marc, she pursed her lips, set her chin, doubled over, and pushed with all her force, sending him flying into the partially filled silo.

"Why you—" He grabbed for her waist, hauling her in with him. Michael and Mandy, caught up in the action, jumped in after them. Kari sputtered and coughed from the strong, pungent odor of the silage. Before she could recover, she realized that she was involved in a giant free-for-all tackle.

"Help me, Kari! Tickle Marc! He's extremely ticklish," Mindy screeched as she struggled to escape her two big brothers.

"Oh ho! A weakness in the armor? And one that can't be reciprocated." Kari giggled and charged into the squirming mass of confusion.

"Oh no you don't!" Marc turned suddenly toward Kari. "If you tickle me, I'll get you back."

"Ah ha, I have you this time. I'm not ticklish!" Kari grinned devilishly, her fingers wiggling in wicked anticipation.

Marc arched one eyebrow as she moved closer. Suddenly he darted forward and stuffed a handful of silage down the back of her shirt.

"Oh, you're going to get it yet, Mr. Marc Wynters. You wait. You'll pay dearly for this one!" Kari writhed about, trying to dislodge the itchy silage.

"And as for you, young lady—" Marc turned on his sister, who wisely took off running for the house and for the safety of her own room.

During breakfast the four of them discussed the accident again, and their course of action.

"I'll stay here with the family as long as you need me," Kari said. "I can close up Grandma Lewis's place as long as I check on it from time to time. Mom will need help running the house, I'm sure. I'll keep my job, of course." Kari replaced the cover on the strawberry jam jar.

"Thanks. I'll be here too. I arranged with the university to take my finals later and to intern with Doc Adams. It will mean driving to Columbus every day and sometimes at night, but with Dad off the line, Michael will need all the help he can get."

Kari beamed at the news. "Great!"

"It took some doing to get clearance for the internship. I did a lot of praying and a whole lot of begging," Marc admitted. "Yvonne wasn't any too pleased, either. I was scheduled to do my internship near her parents' home in Michigan."

"I'm sure that when she thinks it all through, she'll understand." Kari placed the pitcher of milk in the refrigerator. "I'd better check to see if Mindy and Michael are ready for school, or they'll miss their bus."

Marc reached out and caught her arm. "I told them to go back to bed. It won't hurt them to miss school one day. They're both beat."

"I suppose you're right. They've been through a lot in the last twenty-four hours. Speaking of which, I should call and see how your mom and dad are doing." Kari shied away from Marc's grasp.

"I already called while you were making breakfast. They're resting well, and the doctor advises us to do the same. Now come on, let me help you with the dishes; then you go upstairs and get some sleep. And that's an order!"

A dark cloud settled on Kari's face, causing Marc to stop short and reconsider his words. "I mean, I suggest that you get some sleep. Is that better?"

"Much, thank you. Yes, sleep sounds appealing," Kari nodded, her eyes glistening.

"Women!" Marc sputtered as he tossed the dish cloth over the hook.

"Men!" Kari hissed as she ran upstairs to her room.

# Chapter 14
# More Than Second Best

Mom and Dad Wynters fussed when Marc and Kari explained their schedule to organize the house and farm chores while they were hospitalized.

"You can't do that, son." Dad raised up on one elbow and shook his finger at Marc. "You belong back at the university so that you can graduate at the end of the month, and Kari is putting in eight hours every night at the hospital."

"What do you expect to do?" Marc asked. "Lose the farm? Michael can't handle things alone—you know that."

"I'll—I'll—" Dad insisted.

"You'll do as the doctors tell you. Besides, I've made all the arrangements. I'll drive back to the campus for final tests and for the graduation exercises. The neighbors have agreed to cover the daily chores for me the three days I'll be gone. So it's all settled. There's no sense in arguing, is there?" Marc grinned, folding his arms in a self-satisfied stance, reminiscent of Dad Wynters himself.

The doctor released Mom and Dad to go home the morning of the third day after the accident. Each morning after that, Kari looked forward to her favorite time of the day: breakfast with the family. After the meal, and after Mindy and Michael had left for school and Mom had gone upstairs to be with Dad, Marc and Kari shared a quiet time together cleaning the kitchen. They debated everything from government intervention in farming to equal rights for equal pay. They shared their memories and their dreams for the future. Some mornings, only the fact that Kari hadn't slept all night ended their long conversations.

Kari also learned that Marc seldom remembered to put his dirty socks in the hall hamper. Usually, she had to crawl under his bed to find them in order to do his washing, and her nagging didn't seem to change a thing. She learned that he slammed doors when he was angry and that he hated mushrooms. It simultaneously irritated, yet pleased her, when Marc worried over her like a mother hen. "You must be sure to get your sleep. Otherwise you'll never be able to keep up with this hectic schedule," he fussed one morning as Kari added more water to the pot of navy beans soaking on the stove.

"I'm doing fine, Daddy, just fine." She patted his right hand condescendingly. He placed his left hand on top of hers.

"I mean it, Kari. We're a team. I need you. Please take care of yourself."

"I will, I promise." Kari slipped her hand from between Marc's. "How's Yvonne?"

"About the same. She's nagging me to visit her this weekend. She doesn't seem able to understand why I can't."

"Give her time. She's never lived on a farm. And your leaving school came as a big shock, remember?" Kari sponged out the microwave oven as she talked.

Marc leaned against the kitchen counter. "Kari, did you ever make a big mistake and didn't know how to rectify it?"

"Many times." She ran the sponge over the sink and faucets.

"Did you feel that way when you went home last time?"

Her hands shook. "At first I did."

Marc pulled a chair out from the table and sat down. "At first?"

"Yeah, when I found Keith there I almost turned around and came right back." Kari stared out the window for a moment.

"Why didn't you?"

"I've asked myself that question a number of times. But my mother really did need me. And I did a lot of praying while I was there, I can tell you that. Amanda and I spent hours together reading the promises and praying." Kari paused. "I learned a lot about myself when I was home this time. It was almost as if I were an outsider, not really involved. I could view everything from a different perspective."

"Everything?"

"Yeah. I guess it happened when I realized that Sheena's lifestyle was her choice, not mine, and that with God's help I don't need to make the same mistakes she's made." Kari rinsed the sponge. "When I first came to Wisconsin I was rebelliously independent, I guess to escape my environment. Remember? Now it's different, somehow. I feel responsible before God for the decisions I make. Am I making sense?"

"Very much so," Marc said, gazing thoughtfully at Kari, a slight frown furrowing his brow.

"What's the matter? Is my hair freaking you out or something?" Kari asked, running a nervous hand through her curls.

"Uh, no. Everything's fine. Now you head on upstairs for a good day's sleep, ya' hear?"

"Yes, Daddy." Kari laughed nervously.

"And can that 'Daddy' stuff," he scolded, tapping her arm playfully. "I am definitely not your daddy."

"Big brother then?" she teased.

"Uh, maybe for the time being," he answered evasively and strolled from the kitchen.

Kari sighed and bounded up the stairs to her bedroom. Within minutes she was in bed and asleep. Her dreamless state was interrupted as the hall clock gonged four. She could hear the sound of a vacuum cleaner in the room below. "Four o'clock already? It can't be." She jumped from the bed and dashed for the shower. Fifteen minutes later, dressed in blue jeans and a white peasant blouse, Kari bounded down the stairs and into the living room, where Mindy had just finished the vacuuming.

"I'm sorry I overslept. I've got to get those beans baking if we expect to eat supper tonight."

"It's OK." Mindy flicked the dust cloth across the piano keys, her face aglow with satisfaction. "I already started them."

"Why, thank you, Mindy. You didn't have to, you know." Kari hugged her, planting a kiss on the young girl's cheek.

"I know, but Mom came downstairs for a few minutes while Dad was asleep, and she told me what to put in 'em. Ya' know, I kinda like working in the kitchen. I never thought I would. Somehow it's more fun now than it used to be when Mom would make me do it." Mindy hung the dust cloth on a hook in the utility closet. "After she went back upstairs to Daddy, I mixed up a batch of bran muffins too."

"Great. Um-um, they certainly smell good!" Kari sniffed the air.

"Oh, no! I forgot to take them out in time." Mindy dashed for the oven and yanked open the door. "Oh, relief. They're a little browner than I'd have liked them to be, but, well—what do you think?"

Kari smiled at the darkened muffins, recalling her first baking efforts right in this very kitchen less than a year ago. "I think I'd get them out of the tin right away. If the bottoms aren't scorched they'll taste fine."

"Oh, I'm glad." Mindy loosened the muffins and dumped them onto the cooling rack. "Marc and Michael would have teased me unmercifully if they'd burned."

Kari reached for the peach-colored quilted placemats for the supper table. "Hey, don't let those oafs discourage you. You know, Mindy, I once read where it said that there's more Christianity in a hearty loaf of home-made bread than most people realize. I think that goes for bran muffins too," she encouraged. "It's been great having your dad come to the table for the evening meal."

"You bet. Things just don't seem right without him here. Oops! There goes the phone. I'll get it." Mindy ran from the room.

Kari set a water tumbler at each place around the oval table. "Let's see now, baked beans, Mindy's muffins, potato salad, carrot and celery sticks, coleslaw, left over apple pie. Yes, that should take care of it."

"That was Marc. He said he'd be home a little late tonight." Mindy grabbed a handful of paper napkins to place around the table.

"You want to check the baked beans?"

"Sure." Mindy slipped her hands into a pair of oven mittens and removed the bubbling casserole from the oven.

Kari smiled at the familiar sound of Michael dashing up the stairs to shower and change clothes. In five minutes, she'd hear Michael and Mindy helping Dad down the stairs for supper and Mom clucking her concern as she preceded them.

When she entered the kitchen, Mom looked around the room and asked, "Where's Marc?"

Mindy helped her father adjust his cast on a stool beside the table. "Oh, he just called and said he'd be a little late tonight. He didn't say why, but if you ask me, he sounded upset."

"Maybe Doc's thoroughbred mare went into labor," Dad suggested.

"Yeah, maybe." Mindy slipped into her place beside Kari. Throughout the meal, Michael kept the family laughing about his afternoon in the chemistry lab.

After supper Mindy placed the last of the supper dishes in the dishwasher while Kari cleaned the placemats and returned them to the drawer. Marc's truck pulled into the yard as she wrung out the dish cloth. She hurried to the refrigerator to prepare a plate of food for him, but instead of coming to the kitchen as he normally did, he trudged up the stairs, slamming his bedroom door behind him. Mindy looked at Kari and raised one eyebrow. Kari scowled and listened. The only sound from upstairs was the voice of the commentator for the evening TV news drifting down from the master bedroom.

Kari waited for a few minutes, trying to decide what to do. "Should I call to him? Take a plate of food upstairs to him, or just let him be?" She waited a few minutes longer. "I think I need a nice long walk," she said at last. She started the dishwasher and walked into the parlor, where by now Mindy sat curled up in a chair reading a school book. "If Marc decides to eat, I've placed his plate in the refrigerator. A minute and a half in the microwave should be enough to reheat it."

Mindy nodded. "I'll tell him. I'd come with you, except I have a 4-H meeting tonight."

"How are you getting there?" Kari asked as she walked toward the front door.

"Michael arranged for the Currens to pick us up. I realize his generosity is so he can see Cindy Curren, but that's OK by me, as long as I get there."

"Great. You run along and have fun." Kari slung her sweater across one shoulder, grabbed a spare Bible from the stand next to the couch, and sauntered down the front steps. The sun hung low in the sky. She sensed someone watching her as she strolled along the rutted driveway. Turning toward the house, she spotted Marc at his bedroom window and waved, then continued down the road.

A large pebble in her path brought out the little girl in her. She kicked it with her toe. It tumbled ahead along the road. She kicked it again, and again. As usual, her thoughts drifted back to Marc. The easy-going friendship they'd developed over the last few weeks pleased her, and she had to admit to herself that she desired to be more than just a friend, even more than a good friend. "Maybe, in the long run, a friendship is all we'll ever have, Lord, and maybe that is for the best." If so, Kari decided to treasure it for its own sake. After all, she reasoned, most friendships last longer than many romances.

Reaching her favorite rock alongside a giant elm tree at the edge of a hay field, Kari jumped the drainage ditch and settled down at the base of a tree to read a few chapters. She shifted to the far side of the tree so that the sun would not blind her eyes.

"Let's see, Romans 8. Yes, that's where I left off last night," she murmured, turning the gilt-edge pages carefully. "Here we are. Romans 8:14." A honeybee buzzed her face, attracted by her mild perfume. She brushed it aside and read on, pausing occasionally to watch a hawk soaring in the sky.

A crow landed on a dirt clod by the edge of the field and squawked. Kari chuckled to herself as the bird twisted its head, first one way then another, trying to determine if its kingdom remained secure with a human alien perched so close. She returned to her reading—verse 28.

A sudden squeal of delight caused the bird to dart into the air. "Here it is! The verse Mom quotes to me so often! 'We know that all things work together for good to them that love God, to them who are the called according to his purpose.' That's neat, really neat!" She laid the Bible on the ground and stared at the pastoral scene spread out before her. Her mind drifted back over the last two years.

" 'All things work together.' I'm sorry to be so impatient, Lord." Kari leaned her head against the rock. "I want to see things happen *now*—instant answers to my prayers for Sheena, Keith, Marc. And I know that what I think should happen is not necessarily what is best from Your perspective. I do trust You to do what's best for all concerned. Your will, Lord, not mine." A breeze blew her curls across her face. She pushed them back.

The sun dropped closer to the horizon. Stiff from sitting on the unplowed ground, Kari stood and stretched, then planted herself on the giant rock beside the field. She leaned forward, chin in hand, enjoying the solitude. She failed to hear Marc's approach until he stood squarely behind her on the far side of the rock.

"Hi, mind if I join you?" He motioned toward the stone.

She smiled at him. "Help yourself."

He glanced down at her open Bible. "I don't want to interrupt anything."

"Oh no, I finished reading a while back. I was just wool gathering, I guess."

He sat down at the base of the rock, inches from her feet. "From the look on your face, I'd say you had mighty serious thoughts."

Kari reached out automatically to touch the tiny curls swirling around his neck, then drew back, scolding herself for harboring such thoughts. "You don't look to be any too jovial yourself." Kari pursed her lips thoughtfully.

Marc broke a twig and began doodling in the sand. "No, I guess I'm not."

"Anything go wrong over at Doc Adams's place today?"

Marc tensed. "No, not really." His jaw hardened as he stared out at the gathering sunset. Kari breathed a quick prayer and decided to refrain from asking further questions.

Soft mauves, pinks, and yellows dominated the western horizon as the sun dipped from view. They watched in silence as the colors swept slowly across the color spectrum to cool blues and lavenders.

Finally, Marc spoke. "I got a long-distance phone call at Doc's today."

"Oh?" Kari waited impatiently for him to continue.

"From Yvonne."

Kari's eyes widened expectantly, then shaded. "Oh?"

"We argued. She and her parents are planning a big party in our honor. She couldn't understand why I refused to drive to Michigan *right now*. I tried to explain, but she wouldn't listen." He paused.

Kari leaned forward, her chin resting in her hands. "Oh?"

"As usual, she threatened to call off our engagement."

"Oh?"

"This time, I told her to go ahead."

"Oh!" Kari gasped.

Marc's blue eyes turned steel gray. "Is that all you can say? 'Oh'?"

"I'm sorry," Kari began.

"Naw, that's OK. I shouldn't have snapped at you. I've done a lot of thinking about our relationship, mine and Yvonne's. And I guess I've known for a long time that it was less than ideal," Marc admitted. "She appears to be so soft and feminine, you know, all sugar and spice to look at, but with an irrational will beneath the glaze."

"Oh?" Kari started. "I mean—I'm sorry."

But Marc hadn't heard her reply. "I know now that Yvonne would hate living on a farm for the rest of her life. Her idea of a veterinary clinic is a posh little poodle boutique in Detroit suburbia, I'm afraid. Our values are too different."

"I'm sorry." Kari touched his shoulder gently.

For a moment, he looked away. "Well, I guess the change from 'Oh' to 'I'm sorry' is an improvement," he drawled, patting her hand tenderly.

"Life is frustrating, isn't it? Just when we think we have our futures all planned, something happens to change everything." Kari picked up a pebble and tossed it at a large clod of dirt in the road. "I think I understand how you feel, Marc. One time when I thought I'd lost a particularly close friend, another dear friend reminded me that 'all things do work together for good to them that love the Lord.' I was just reading it. Here it is. Romans 8:28."

"Yes, I know the verse well. But you don't completely understand, I'm afraid. I feel hurt, yes, but more from the embarrassment of a broken engagement than from losing Yvonne."

Kari noted the tight hunch in Marc's shoulders, the tired lines in his forehead. Gently, skillfully, she massaged his aching shoulders. "A broken engagement is far better than a broken marriage."

He straightened, giving her better access to his shoulders and neck.

"Really! During the last few weeks I've been so confused."

Kari worked her thumbs into a particularly stubborn knot at the base of his neck.

"It's late," he said a moment later. "You'll have to be getting ready for work soon, and suddenly I'm starving." He pulled her to her feet, holding her at arms' length for a second or two longer than necessary. "Thanks. Thanks so much for being here tonight, and for being such a good friend." Marc leaned forward and kissed her on the tip of her nose and looked into her eyes. She held his gaze.

"Did anyone ever tell you that you look like a wood nymph in the moonlight?" he whispered. "I'm afraid that if I turn my back, you'll disappear." His mouth creased into a teasing grin, but his eyes remained wide and questioning. A resounding growl from his stomach broke the spell. They both laughed.

"Food! The master demands food!" Kari skipped across the ditch to the roadbed.

"Wait!" he called, stumbling on a large clod of dirt, but she continued running toward the house.

"As tempting as it is, I won't be his rebound love," she determined. "No way! As much as I care for him, I won't be second best. Lord, this may sound selfish, but I want all of his heart, not just a bruised corner."

# Chapter 15
# Maybe a Lifetime

Kari stood folding the last load of wash when Marc strolled into the laundry room. "Want to go with me to check on Grandma Lewis's place? Dad said he saw someone nosing around over there the other morning."

By now Mom had worked herself back into the daily routine, leaving Kari with extra time on her hands, which Marc usually managed to fill. Kari cautioned herself not to take his attentions too seriously. She was surprised, however, that he didn't mention Yvonne more often. "Maybe it hurts too much," she reasoned.

They jumped into the pickup and drove to the empty farmhouse. As the truck pulled to a stop, Kari jumped out and dashed to the porch to unlock the front door. Marc grabbed her arm before she could open the door. "You'd better wait until we check for intruders before you go inside."

After Marc checked the inside of the house Kari toured the place while Marc inspected the barn and the sheds. "This place needs a once-over badly," she declared as she ran her hand along the top of the mantel piece. Kari removed a dust mop from Grandma's utility closet and dusted the highly polished hardwood floors. Then she ran a cloth over the dark oak stands beside the couch and lounge chair, singing as she dusted. Since Marc still hadn't returned from the out buildings, she decided to give the stairs a once-over also. She dusted them one at a time, starting at the top and backing down.

As her foot landed on the ground floor, she bumped into a solid object. "Gotcha!" Marc laughed, grabbing her by the waist and twirling her around. She landed in a heap on the couch. He loomed over the back of the couch grinning at her discomfort.

She gasped, her heart still pounding from his surprise attack. "Don't you *ever* do that again! You scared the daylights out of me. I didn't hear you come into the house."

"Sorry about that." His dimples belied the insincerity of his apology.

She jumped to her feet. "I'll bet. I'll just bet!" She eyed him suspiciously.

"Why, may I ask, are you cleaning this place today? It will be dusty again by next week."

"That's a great attitude. Why milk the cows? You'll only have to milk them again tonight," Kari replied.

He laughed at her analogy. "It's not the same, though I do see your point."

Kari tipped her head forward acknowledging his apology. "Anyway, to answer your question, the real estate agent called Friday and said that he planned to take a potential buyer through the house tomorrow or the next day. I just thought it might help if I touched things up a bit." She twirled around slowly and sighed. "I'll hate to see the old place go. I feel quite attached to it. I mean, where would you find a huge fireplace like that, all made of rocks taken from the river flowing by your back door? The entire place is so—so warm and . . ."

Kari halted midsentence as Marc stepped up beside her, gripped her waist, and drew her to his side. ". . . and inviting?"

"I was going to say 'homey'," she stammered.

He brushed a stray curl from her neck, weaving it back into her hair clasp. "You belong in a home like this. This room is really you."

"Why, thank you, Marc. That was a sweet thing to say."

Marc whispered in her ear, "I like being sweet to you."

Kari turned and smiled. "Marc, not yet. It's too soon after Yvonne, at least for me."

"Look, I admit it, we got off to a rough start—you with your fear of Keith and me with my fear of being tied down. And then, the first thing I do is get myself tied down to another. Like in the Old Testament, I exchanged gold for brass. Talk about poor judgment!"

"Then there's the bullying!" Kari teased.

For an instant, Marc's temper flared. "No fair! I've really tried to respect your wishes and not strong-arm you into my way of thinking."

"I'm sorry. You *have* tried, I can tell. I shouldn't tease about that. During the last few weeks you've taught me a few unsavory things about myself. Like my temper and my stubbornness."

"And your ability to misinterpret my motives," Marc added.

Kari tilted her head to one side and arched her eyebrow teasingly. "I'd hate to forfeit this great friendship we've built. After all, regardless of how many women you propose to during your lifetime, I plan on being your friend both here and for eternity, like it or not." Her smile faded as Marc leaned forward, his lips gently touching hers. Kari's breath caught as Marc released her.

"A friendship kiss, right?" he drawled.

"Yeah, sure, a friendship kiss," she replied, her mind confused by a string of tender memories from the past year.

Kari drew away slightly and looked at the floor. Mark released his hold on her arms.

"Marc," she began, "my intellect tells me your heart is now free, but my emotions fear that you're only on parole. Can you understand?" He nodded and strode out to the truck.

From that moment on, Marc kept his distance, ever solicitous, ever helpful, and ever a friend. Kari watched and waited, uncertain she'd ever know for sure that Yvonne was totally in the past.

On the weekend of Marc's graduation, Kari agreed to stay with Dad so that the rest of the family could go to the ceremonies. All weekend, Kari prayed that she would be able to accept the possibility that Marc would see Yvonne again and might decide to renew their relationship.

When the family returned from Michigan late Monday afternoon, Mindy talked of nothing else. "You should have seen Yvonne's parents' graduation present to her! A brand new, silver-toned Mercedes with genuine, pearl grey, leather seats."

"And the instruments on the dashboard could fly a 747," Michael added. "Wow, what a car! Someday I'm going to buy myself one just like it."

During the following week Marc seemed aloof, preoccupied. The subject of Yvonne suddenly dropped from everyone's interest. No one mentioned the girl or her car. Kari felt as if she would burst from curiosity if someone didn't say something soon.

On Friday morning, as Kari pulled into the driveway, she spotted a new, silver-gray Mercedes parked by the front door. Her stomach knotted. She leaned her head against the steering wheel and prayed for strength. "Oh, dear God, not now. I played by the rules. I stayed out of arm's reach while he was pledged to her. Why, why does she have to come back into his life just as we seem to be getting somewhere?"

She ran her fingers through her hair, releasing the ponytail holder. "I'm sorry, Lord. Here I go questioning Your wisdom again. Forgive me. And keep forgiving me, since I seem to be such a slow learner."

Kari slipped through the front door and headed directly to her room. When Kari was halfway up the stairs, Mom called from the kitchen. "Kari, is that you? We're all at the breakfast table ready for worship. Do you want to join us?"

Kari bit her lip. "Talk about terrible timing!" she muttered, then called back, "Sure, Mom, let me dump my things on my bed, and I'll be right down."

Kari felt the tension in the air instantly as she entered the kitchen. An extra chair had been added next to Marc for Yvonne. Yvonne sent Kari a self-satisfied smile, as if to say, "He's mine, sweety, hands off."

Kari read the message, sat down in the remaining empty chair, and forced an exuberant grin across her face. "What a night! Sorry to keep everybody waiting," she said, trying to sound matter-of-fact. She glanced about the table as quickly as possible. When Kari finally built up the courage to look toward Marc, his eyes sent her such a pleading look that she choked on her swallow of milk.

As soon as it was polite to do so, Kari escaped to her room. She sat on the edge of the bed and opened her Bible to one of her favorite promises. Her hopes sank when she heard Marc and Yvonne's voices outside her window. They got into Yvonne's car and drove off. "Lord, I can't believe he's doing this to us," she sobbed. After a long and agonizing prayer, Kari fell exhausted onto her bed and was soon fast asleep.

That evening, as Kari prepared for work, she noted that Yvonne and Marc had not returned home since morning. She headed for the hospital with a heavy heart. Throughout the night she made her rounds from room to room, forcing herself to smile, to be cheerful. The night dragged on into the wee hours of the morning. Anne, the other nurse assigned to Kari's floor, talked almost without stopping. Kari found it difficult to pay attention.

"Then I fixed a platter of strychnine sandwiches and a pot of arsenic tea for them."

Kari nodded thoughtfully as if waiting for her to continue.

Anne stared in disbelief, then giggled. "Did you hear what I said?"

"Of course. You said you made sandwiches and tea for the two of you."

Anne giggled again. "I said, 'I fixed a platter of strychnine sandwiches and a pot of arsenic tea'." She paused, and her eyes teased Kari. "OK, where were you just now?"

"I'm sorry. I guess I just have a lot on my mind tonight." Kari's eyes belied the turmoil she struggled to hide.

Anne extended her hand to Kari's. "Anything I can help you with?"

"No, not really."

Kari jumped when the buzzer rang from room 231. "Oh, Mr. Peters needs me. Probably his IV is acting up again. I've had the worst time with it tonight!"

Kari moved mechanically from one task to the next until the seven-to-three shift arrived. Anne volunteered to give report for her, enabling Kari to check out sooner. Kari hurried out to her car and hopped in. Suddenly a man sat up in the back seat of her car. Kari whirled. "Marc!" she screamed.

"Hi, give me a lift?"

Kari stared at him, her composure shot. "Where did *you* come from?"

He got out of the back seat, into the front. "You know what? That back seat isn't made for sleeping."

"How long have you been here?" Kari fumbled with her key. It refused to go into the ignition.

"Oh, probably since midnight," he drawled.

Kari's mouth dropped, and she stared at him. "But . . . but . . . but . . . Where's Yvonne?"

Marc rubbed his eyes and yawned. "Oh, probably back in Michigan by now." He leaned back against the seat and closed his eyes. Kari started the engine and drove out of the parking lot down Main Street.

Marc opened one eye to look across at Kari. "Mind stopping for breakfast? I know a great little place a few miles out of town."

"On the way home?" Kari questioned. "I've never seen any eating place there."

Marc pulled the car visor down to keep the sun out of his eyes. "Sure 'nough. I've eaten there many times."

Kari clicked her tongue and agreed. "Well, OK." She drove on, waiting for Marc to say something about Yvonne—anything, but he appeared to be catching a catnap instead. She drove on several miles without saying anything.

"Marc Wynters! What kind of game are you playing?" she asked as they neared home. "There isn't any restaurant on this part of the highway. There's just Grandma's turn off here, then home."

He sat up and leaned forward. "That's right; turn here."

"Where?" Kari demanded.

"Here!"

"Why?"

"Because I said so."

"Marc, this doesn't make sense."

"Does everything have to make sense?"

Kari sighed, her eyes reflecting impatience and fatigue. "Marc, I'm too tired to play games. This is Grandma's driveway. I want to go home. I had a rough night."

"So did I, come to think of it," Marc drawled. "Aw Kari, I wanted you to check out the house I'm planning to buy. It won't take long," Marc pleaded with his best little-boy innocence.

Kari froze at the wheel. "What? You're buying Grandma Lewis's house?"

"Wait until you see what I've done to the inside. I want to get your opinion on the changes I've made."

Kari stopped the car directly in front of the house. Marc leaped from the car and bounded toward the front door. Kari's heart lurched as she tried to picture Yvonne standing in the doorway welcoming visitors to their honeymoon cottage.

Pasting a game smile on her face, Kari climbed out of the car and walked to the open door. When she reached the top step, Marc swept into a grand Sir Walter Raleigh bow, bidding her to enter.

Instead, she stopped to look at him. "Marc, when did you decide to buy Grandma's place?"

He looked toward the sky. "A little over a week ago."

"Oh." Kari blanched. She wondered if he made his decision before or after their last visit here. The visit that had almost changed her mind— almost.

"Now, will you please step into my parlor?"

Kari mumbled, "Said the spider to the . . ." She stopped midsentence. Spread out on a blanket before the lighted fireplace was a lavish meal. "Where? How?" she stuttered.

Marc laughed. "I now understand how Esau must have felt. I almost had to sell my birthright to my little sister for this meal. Mindy agreed to fix the food and bring it over early this morning. Didn't she do a great job?"

Kari coughed and sputtered. "Well, yes, but it's too bad Yvonne isn't here to enjoy it with you."

Marc flung back his head in a hearty laugh. "Yvonne? Why should I want to bring *her* here?"

Confused, Kari weighed Marc's words against her own conclusions. They didn't balance out somehow. She dared not allow the weights to fall in her favor. Her disappointment would be too great should she be wrong. She had to be sure—very, very sure.

Strolling to her side, Marc placed his arm around her and led her to the food. "My dearest Kari, I planned this breakfast long before Yvonne showed up yesterday. Her inconvenient arrival only solidified in my mind a decision I'd already made."

"But . . . I . . . what . . . ?" Kari sputtered, unable to speak coherently.

Marc drew her toward the fireplace, setting her down on the footstool. "Now, my dear, I face the more difficult task, that of convincing you of the fact."

"Of what fact?"

"That I love you. That I have loved you for a very long time, and that I hope you will love me in return, or at least are willing to try." Marc knelt beside the footstool.

"But what about Yvonne?" Kari insisted.

Marc tilted Kari's chin with his hand. "Yvonne drove up here yesterday in an effort to win me back. But she didn't stand a chance, I'm afraid. The girl back home had already wormed her way into my heart."

Dazed and confused, Kari glanced about the room as her mind began to decipher Marc's words.

"You must have known how hard I tried to fight it last summer. I actually convinced myself for a time that I wanted to be free. I chased after Yvonne, thinking she was more pliable, more responsive to me. I was wrong," Marc growled. "To be perfectly honest, she turned out to be spoiled rotten. I was getting to where I couldn't stand the thought of hearing another, 'Marky,' spoken from her lips. I guess I learned that all that glitters is not gold."

"But—" Kari interrupted.

"Sssh, sometimes you talk too much. Let me finish. When I found Keith accosting you, I came unglued. Only the grace of God kept me from tearing him apart. Then this month. It's been fabulous. I've lived for the times during the day when we could be together, talking and laughing, even arguing." Tears glistened in Marc's eyes. "If I'm rushing you, I apologize."

Kari tenderly cupped Marc's face in her hands. He was so kind, so patient with her. She tried to speak, but the words stuck in her throat. Her eyes brimmed with tears.

"No, don't cry," he begged. "How could I have blown this? I've prayed about it for days. I not only love you deeply, but you're also my very dearest friend. I wouldn't hurt you for the world."

Kari pressed her index finger against his lips and grinned. "Sssh!

Sometimes, *you* talk too much. Besides, I don't reason logically on an empty stomach."

Marc brightened. "Hmmph! Is that to my advantage or not?"

"Well, if you want it, you'll have lots of time to find out." Kari poured orange juice from the pitcher into the tumblers.

"A lifetime maybe?" Marc suggested.

Kari paused, looked down into the glass, then smiled over the rim. "Quite possibly," she answered. "Quite possibly."